BLOOD OF POWER

UNREDEEMED

A.R. LEGGETT ©2006

ISBN: 978-0-578-02460-8

Writersblock1717@hotmail.com

2

Thank you to my brothers and sisters of AGR
Your help and support is greatly appreciated.
And to my family for their encouragement...
Peace and Light
A.R.

CHAPTER ONE

Tempest stood in the center of her new office and frowned. I must be crazy, she thought. What am I doing here?

A cool breeze blew through the open window and, chilled, she hugged herself. Past taunts filled her mind, painful echoes. Crazy Tempest, Crazy Tempest! Shivering, she suppressed those memories, took a deep breath, and examined her surroundings.

The small room was intimate and dimly lit, its single large window covered with a heavy curtain of beige lace. Daylight filtered through to form dappled shadows upon the walls, bare except for one simple print of a vast lake and mountains.

In the center of the room stood an oval table covered with a lace tablecloth matching the curtain. A white candle, denoting good and positive energy, burned at its center. Myrrh incense smoked in a small brass bowl to its right, adding its rich fragrance to the still air. To the left a thick black candle stood to offer protection.

Tempest placed a china cup and saucer opposite her and sat before the white candle. After taking three deep, cleansing breaths, she made a mental inventory of her appearance. Would it have the desired effect?

Her dark auburn hair hung loose in a cascade of waves to her waist. A thin strand of pearls adorned her brow, which kept wayward strands out of her face. She wore a turquoise -hued dress, very native in its imagery. Blessed with dark skin and almond eyes of her Native American ancestors, and auburn hair and heart shaped face of her Scottish ancestors, all that was required was black eyeliner to look mystical and wise.

Reverently, Tempest lit the black candle and uttered a prayer to the Creator, thanking him for her gifts and asking for wisdom to use them wisely.

Maybe she really was crazy and not wise at all. After all, she was twenty six years of age, an excellent medical secretary, and willing to work at a modest tea room after hours without pay.

Smiling, she recalled the incredulous look Maggie, the owner of the tea room, gave her a mere three days earlier. Pushing her hair out of her face, Tempest had entered the tea room and walked right up to the desk to address Maggie, who visibly pulled away from her.
Undaunted, she'd blurted, "I know things. Feel things. I need to learn how to control it, and to use it. But I don't want to make money from it. That feels wrong to me."

Maggie frowned, and Tempest knew instantly the woman took offense to her money comment. She also knew the other woman's son was in serious trouble and would definitely serve time. Other, less significant secrets revealed themselves.

Maggie huffed," How do I know you're any good? I have a reputation to maintain. You don't seem gifted." With a sweeping gaze she looked at Tempest's attire, lemon yellow linen suit, skirt just below the knee, sensible walking shoes, and scarce make up. Maggie actually shook her head.

Tempest felt so much in those few seconds, hostility, anger, and jealousy. Maggie was a bitter individual. " Listen," Tempest blurted," You're really depressed right now. Your son, I believe he's twenty two years old, is up on drug charges, and will go to jail for a short time. Don't be upset. He'll learn a lot in there and come out a better person. Your mother hasn't spoken to you since...last Monday, because you want her to co-sign for a new tea room. She doesn't trust your judgment. Oh yes! You've been celibate for eighteen months...and you hate it!"

Maggie froze, her mouth dropped open.

Tempest smiled. She began working the next day.

After only three days, it felt more like weeks. She spent her nights with depressed people sitting opposite her, desperate to know which path to take. Most nurtured dreams of winning the lottery, or falling in love. Tempest just wanted them to embrace life. This job was quite an eye opener.   In between clients, she sat back in her chair, listening. Through the open window she could hear soft laughter, car doors slamming. Closing her eyes, she tried to visualize what was taking place outside. Ahh...a couple. A happy couple had just enjoyed a great meal in a restaurant. The woman was in love and,..hmm...he wasn't.

Tempest quickly realized there were a lot of unhappy people in Boston, a major loss of hope. She revealed inadequate glimpses to her customers, peeks at their future, but was unable to really fix their problems. Yet...Maggie sent more and more clients to her. Men and women left her office smiling. It was puzzling. Tempest brushed a strand of hair from her face and frowned. The fact she was insecure, lonely, and just as confused as her clients made her feel empty.

Inhaling deeply to steady herself, Tempest prepared for the gentleman due at any moment. Frowning, she focused on the candle burning before her. All she knew about her expected client was his name...Michael Rivendi. He was a blank page and it was up to her to write a biography through her perceptions.

" I wish I could feel them before they show up," she thought aloud. Tempest hated the first meeting the most, when the unknown was at its maximum. She mused about this, just as with a soft knock at her door, a man entered. At least six feet tall with the slim, well toned physique of a runner, his pale blonde hair fell to his shoulders, not exactly the fashion these days. He sat opposite her with an air of confidence and focused vivid blue eyes on her face.

Tempest's breath caught in her throat. She felt strong sexual attraction to this man. It gripped her unaware, making it hard to breathe. Confused and surprised, she mumbled, "Would you like some tea Mr. Rivendi?"

Even as she spoke, the arousal that permeated her began to change somehow, not quite as pleasant but just as intense. The man leaned toward her and instinctively, Tempest cringed, feeling actual heat emanate from him.

"Call me Michael...and no, the tea won't be necessary."

His voice! It was silk and broken glass. Tempest recoiled consumed by a new emotion, revulsion. Evil wafted from him like a noxious cloud. Fumes reeking of foul deeds, and,..secrecy. Repulsed, she leaned away from her handsome client and closed her eyes in a vain attempt to sort the feelings assaulting her. All she could feel was lack of light, emptiness. It permeated his being. She'd never encountered this before! Bile actually rose in her throat. Every instinct urged her to flee. When she forced her eyes open, squinting because of an encroaching headache, he was gone. She was relieved. The room felt clean again.

Shaken, Tempest stared at the bright candles, aware of sweat cooling on her brow and upper lip. As her senses cleared, she realized what an error she'd made. If anyone needed help, Michael Rivendi did!

She raced out to the reception area. It was empty except for Maggie at the desk.

"Maggie...did you see Mr. Rivendi leave?"

Two other psychics walked past her, laughing comfortably. They nodded, handing a roll of receipts to Maggie, before continuing to their offices.

"Did he leave, Maggie?"

"Oh, sorry." Maggie placed the papers in a drawer before focusing on Tempest. "Michael Rivendi? He hasn't come yet."

"What? He just left my office. I owe him an apology."

"What are you talking about? He never showed up. I've been right here so I should know. Are you alright?"

Confused, Tempest said rather shakily, "But I saw him, a tall handsome man with long blonde hair and bright blue eyes."

Maggie shook her head. " No one came in looking like that, and I haven't left this desk. Maybe you fell asleep."

Tempest knew she had not fallen asleep. He'd been there alright. Noticing the concerned look on Maggie's face, she forced a smile on her own, and brightly waved a hand. "Sorry I bothered you."

"It's alright, honey."

Maggie lifted a pink slip of paper from her desk and handed it to Tempest. "On the way to your office could you stop at no.19 and give this to Paul? He has a cancellation."

"No problem." Taking the paper, Tempest headed down the carpeted hallway. She had no doubt Maggie was telling the truth, about not seeing Michael Rivendi. Tempest couldn't think of another entrance, and why would he sneak in anyway? What of Michael himself? How could she want to go to bed with a man, yet detest the idea of touching him? She trembled inwardly.

Pulling herself from her thoughts, Tempest stopped at office no.19,and gently knocked.

"Come in!"

Entering the office, she was struck by the cheerfulness of the room. It was bright and airy, scented with sage. Nice. The man seated at the table got up and gave her a smile as welcoming as the office.

"Hi! Tempest right, room seven?"

She nodded, taken back by his demeanor, so in contrast to the man she met earlier. Tempest quickly handed him the note.

He perused her with the darkest eyes she'd ever seen. Heavy black curls covered his head with abandon. "I'd say Blackfoot, Cherokee and Scottish."

"What!?"

"Your heritage. But swap the pearls for a headband. Will make a better impression on clients. They love the Native American thing."

"Excuse me?" Tempest felt insulted, but he was right about her heritage.

With a broad grin, he continued, " I have a bit of Cherokee, but I'm still your basic Hebrew black man. Ha!"

Tempest tried not to grin, but she couldn't help herself. "Are you psychic,..or crazy?"

"Both. My clients are crazier though. Nice meeting you, at last."

"Same here." She turned to leave, but he called out.

"Tempest, you're different. Why are you here?"

Curious, she spun around. "What do you mean?"

Paul approached her, the smile absent from his face. "I mean you're serious power. This isn't the place for you."

Dismissing his words, she shook her head. "Flattery is wasted on me. I can see you're used to women falling at your feet."

"No. Falling into my bed. And I never flatter."

"I see." Tempest turned away, then froze when he touched her shoulder. There was a warm sensation. For a fleeting moment, she wondered what it would feel like to be touched by Michael Rivendi,..man of darkness.

"Have you had dinner?"

"Yes."

"No,..you haven't. You're starved."

As if in answer, her stomach growled.

He released her. "Care to get a bite to eat? I'm starved too."

Tempest relaxed, and realized she liked him. The only negative she could grasp was he had a big ego. But the man might even deserve that. "Alright. A quick bite. I have an 8:00 appointment."

"Fine. It's just after seven. Let's go."

As Tempest followed him down the hall and out the door, she reminded herself never to lie to this man again. He would know.

CHAPTER TWO

To her surprise, Tempest enjoyed listening to the easy flow of Paul's conversation. There was a soothing quality to his voice, like a lullaby, causing her to relax and forget about the strange meeting with Michael. She regretted having to end the meal and return to work. Drinking the last of her soda, and giving him an apologetic smile, Tempest blurted, "I'd better get back to work. It's almost eight."

Paul motioned for the waiter and the check. "I wondered what sort of person you were," he stated, a tiny grin on his face. "You aren't very sociable at work. In at six, gone by nine thirty. In your office the entire time. Like clock work."

"Well. What kind of person do you think I am, now?"

The waiter approached and Paul quickly paid the bill. Looking at her studiously, he hesitated. "I'm not sure. You're a great listener, but you don't talk much. My impressions are vague, and I suppose that's how you want it."

Grinning, Tempest stood and stated, on the way to the exit, "I can tell you this much about me. I'm never late for an appointment. We need to hurry."

As Paul caught up to her she teased," Being prompt is a habit you should cultivate."

His boyish grin warmed her, another surprise. Her emotions obviously were out of whack today!

Maggie looked up when they entered the front office, barely able to hide her surprise. Looking at Paul, she motioned for him to approach the desk. "Mona is hosting a psychic party on Saturday, and wants to know if you'll be one of the guests. She got an okay from four others, but really wants you there. Money looks good."

"Tomorrow,.. I'm free. Mag, what is it? Readings and cards,..what?"

"Everything. But no seance tricks. I know Mona hates that!"

"Seance...TRICKS?," Tempest was appalled. "What kind of tricks,.. Who is that unethical?"

Paul was surprised by her reaction. "Lots of people, but not I."

"I didn't think Maggie allowed trickery from us."

Maggie's sigh was full of exasperation. "I didn't mean to offend your tender sensibilities. But even you must know a few tricks of the trade! No one is one hundred percent."

Tempest glared at her. Tricks. No wonder people were so disgusted when they saw psychic ability. She could still remember the reaction of friends who'd seen some of her ability. Painful rejection, and doubt.

"People can't expect you to always be one hundred percent. But if you can't read them, you just tell them so," she persisted.

Maggie lost her patience. "Hey perfect miss! Some people depend on this for a living. They don't have day jobs. They can't afford to turn people away and lose money. Don't preach to me about being the perfect, ethical psychic. You have a job to fall back on, this is your hobby. For others,.. This is their life!"

Struggling to regain her composure and not retaliate, Tempest looked Maggie right in the eye. "These people pay for help. If they don't get it they're being cheated. Anyone can guess a name, or let clients reveal their own needs and problems, but that's cheating them out of hard earned money."

Paul clasped Tempests hand, flashing a warning look at Maggie at the same time. Tempest felt him gently massage her palm with his thumb. "Drop this," he whispered near her ear, "Your customer will be here any minute."

Feeling the anger drain from her, she nodded and pulled away. Just then the door opened and an elderly business woman entered. She walked up to the desk and asked for Tempest.

Pasting a smile on her face, she turned to the woman and greeted, "Hello. I'm Tempest. You're right on time. Come with me."

She led the woman to her office, feeling Paul's approval as he watched them go down the hall.

Tempest blew out the candle, laid her head on the table, and closed her eyes. She had to go home, but didn't want to. At least here she felt useful, but at home...well, home was a lonely place. Only one month since the laughter stopped. Since fragrant hot dinners ended, and the smell of baked pies. One month since her parents had died needlessly on the expressway, victims of a drunk driver who'd fallen asleep at the wheel. Tears filled her eyes. The raw wound their absence created pulsed with agony. Her tears wet her arms.

She wanted to move but so much of them remained in the house. As if they still lived in the furniture, the walls, everywhere. But it was closing time so she had to face going home once more. The home that was a shrine to a dead man and woman who could show her love no more.

Wiping her tears away, she rose and motivated herself to go. The others had gone already, except for Maggie, who still tallied the days intake of cash, and checked tomorrows schedules.

Tempest waved and proceeded to walk past her, but Maggie motioned for her to come to the desk. "Come here dear, we need to talk."

Tempest didn't want this talk. She considered rushing outside, but didn't want to be so childish. Instead, she walked over and stood before her boss.

"We need to come to an understanding, Tempest. What happened today was inexcusable. You attacked me. This is my shop. I make the rules. How a psychic conducts themselves reflects on me, after all. If a customer is dissatisfied, they won't come back. So I select my psychics

carefully. You assumed I select tricksters, but I never said that.
Remember, you chose me. You came to me, and admitted there is much
you don't know. Why judge others for their methods and knowledge?
Some are more gifted than others. I'm aware that you are very gifted."

Sighing, Tempest thought, what a day. "I didn't mean to judge.
It's just that so many consider psychics phony tricksters, liars, cheats,
gypsies. I want more people to realize that these gifts do exist, then
they'd be accepting of people like us."

Maggie grinned at her . "So..our little Tempest has an injured past.
Teased,..maybe called a witch because of her,..gifts. A little girl who
knew the power of words or saw someone's death, and was scorned for
it. Sweetie, such things are commonplace, don't you know? What you
call a gift, many call a curse."

Commonplace? Tempest hated any memory of her childhood. What
gave others the right to be cruel? "Okay Maggie, I get your drift. No
more judging from me."

Before Maggie could respond, Tempest quickly walked outside.

Park street was empty, its many specialty shops closed for the night.
She peered into the window of her favorite clothing shop. Mannequins
stared back at her through the tinted glass, their lifeless eyes sparkling
eerily from reflected street light. Oddly, they reminded Tempest of
Michael, her strange visitor. How did he get past Maggie, and what did

he want?

She walked faster than usual toward her green volkswagon, parked a block away. Across the street stood neatly clipped hedges along an aged brick wall, which protected the dark interior of the Public Commons? This park within the city bustled with business people, and the homeless during the day, but at night all that was visible behind the wall was shadow, and movements caused by the wind in the trees. For some reason it frightened Tempest tonight. A light chill traced her spine. Reaching her car, she peered inside before opening the door, a precaution she always took. Satisfied no one lurked within, she giggled nervously, opened the door, and slid in.

A small card was lodged under the windshield wipers. She studied it, not able to read the writing, then reached through her window to dislodge it. It was a business card. Michael Rivendis' name was printed boldly in gold script and below it the address to a shop in Brookline called the 'Odds and Ends'. Turning it over, she saw his neat handwriting inviting her to a party he was hosting there tomorrow night. The card felt hot in her grip.

Tempest dropped it on the passenger seat and locked the doors. So many thoughts tumbled through her mind. How did he know her car? What did he want from her? Most of all,..why did he feel so negative? Glancing down at the card, she frowned, puzzled.

" What do you want with me Michael?"

The music blasting in the back room was borderline aggravating. The thin voices of a new rock band cried out a litany of promises and hate. Michaels grin held no mirth or warmth. He closed his eyes for a second before shouting, " Turn that shit off!" Immediately, silence reigned.

Michael Rivendi shuffled his tarot cards and carefully laid them on the counter. He studied the placement of the cards, then grinned. Good. Very good. She would come. That would be the first step.

Two young women sauntered from the back room, stood at his side, and studied the cards on the counter. They were exceptionally beautiful, almost glowing with youth. One, a blonde no more than seventeen, burst into laughter. The other girl smacked her with such venom it knocked the blonde to the floor.

Jumping to her feet, she gave Michael a frightened glance before rushing into the room in the rear. Soft sobs could be heard.

Michael looked at the remaining girl with a radiant smile. Tenderly, he touched her dark hair, then with lightening speed, his smile became a snarl as he encircled her slender neck with both hands. He squeezed, and watched her expression while increasing the pressure. She turned red, then a mottled hue of gray and pink. He ignored her desperate clawing at his hands, and suddenly released her. She fled the same path the blonde had taken, gasping noisily.

Michael smiled again, and returned his attention to his cards.

The music blasting in the back room was borderline aggravating. Thin voices of a new rock band, cried out a litany of promises and hate. Michael's grin held no mirth or warmth. He closed his eyes for a second before shouting, "Turn that shit off!" Immediately, silence reigned.

Michael Rivendi shuffled his tarot cards and carefully laid them on the counter. He studied the placement of the cards, then grinned. Good. Very good. She would come. That would be the first step.

Two young women sauntered from the back room, stood at his side, and studied the cards on the counter. They were exceptionally beautiful, almost glowing with youth. One, a blonde no more than seventeen, burst into laughter. The other girl smacked her with such venom it knocked the blonde to the floor.

Jumping to her feet, she gave Michael a frightened glance before rushing into the room in the rear. Soft sobs could be heard.

Michael looked at the remaining girl with a radiant smile. Tenderly, he touched her dark hair, then with lightening speed, his smile became a snarl as he encircled her slender neck with both hands. He squeezed, and watched her expression while increasing the pressure. She turned red, then a mottled hue of gray and pink. He ignored her desperate clawing at his hands, and suddenly released her. She fled the same path the blonde had taken, gasping noisily.

Michael smiled again, and returned his attention to his cards.

CHAPTER THREE

Tempest readied herself for bed. After a relaxing shower, she slipped
into a plain cotton shift, and sat before her computer. It was the focal
point of her scarcely furnished livingroom. A fold out couch and two
chairs with matching upholstery sat along the walls.
One dusty potted plant managed to thrive in one corner. An expensive
Persian rug lay in the center of the room, obviously out of place. The
entire wall at the front of the house, where her computer desk was
situated, was a huge bookcase filled with volumes of medical books, and
historical accounts. Her mother had loved history.

To avoid thinking about that, Tempest filed some medical records
needed for work on Monday, and typed a few replies to medical patients,
who had asked for accident forms. Last, she typed and faxed the referral
her boss had asked for, regarding another doctor on staff.

While the fax machine hummed, she looked at her surroundings, and
felt her heart clench. Before the deaths of her parents, this room had
been full of character. Artwork gathered during many vacations around
the world, had sat in full view. Proud fertility statues from Peru,
Mandalas from reservations in Arizona, and Mexico. Although she
stored their furniture and trappings away, it felt as if their essence filled

the very air. Would she ever stop missing them, the laughter and loving advice?

After shutting her computer off, Tempest padded barefoot across gleaming wood floors, and collapsed into bed where her tears would lull her to sleep.

Tempest looked up from her coffee, and smiled at Paul. He stood in her office with a hopeful, little boy expression on his handsome face. It was nice to have someone come and greet her on a Saturday morning. "So Tempest. Why don't you attend this party tonight and help out? Mona is afraid to ask you herself."
She wanted to say yes, but wasn't there something else she was supposed to do this Saturday? Oh yes, Michael's party. Should she go?

Tempest had an idea, and grinning, she replied," I'll go and help out if you make me a promise, that you go to another party with me afterwards."

He sat across from her, obviously intrigued. "Alright. Where are we going?"

For a second she examined the neat, precise braids taming his curly hair. Excellent work, obviously done by a woman. When she looked into his eyes they twinkled, his brows raised, almost as if he'd read her thoughts. She broke the spell. "The party is in Brookline, at a shop called Odds and Ends."

" I know the place. They sell all the mystical trappings. Crystal balls, herbs, wands, stuff like that. New age."

Surprised, she asked, " Do you know Michael Rivendi?"

For a while, Paul didn't answer. He shifted in the chair. When he did reply, it was very softly. " I know of the man. Has quite a reputation. But no, can't say I know him."

"Oh,...what kind of reputation?" Tempest tried to pick up on his thoughts, but he kept her at bay somehow.

Abruptly, Paul stood up, his hands clenched. " I don't gossip. I'll go to his party with you. Make up your own mind about him then. Mona's psychic party starts at six, and you can ride with me."

She started to tell him she had a car, but he was already gone. A bit of a chill hung in the air. It was more than clear that Paul didn't like, or approve of Mr. Rivendi!"

CHAPTER FOUR

Mona lived in a small house located in the old world, elite area of Fenway Park. It sat in a cul de sac, neatly guarded by shrubs and stunted trees. Very private, despite the bustle of the area with its movie theatre , shops and bars.

Tempest relaxed as Paul pulled into a tiny parking space with ease. She envied the way he handled his Nissan, as if it was an old friend that

would never fail him. Driving wasn't her favorite pastime.

He leaned across her to open the door, and she was instantly aware of his scent,..something natural,..not overly fragrant like most colognes. "Well, are you ready for this?"

She thought about it a second. It was the first time she'd actually have to work in a crowd, and it scared her. Taking a deep breath, she replied, "Ready as I'll ever be."

People were already gathered inside. Candles sparkled everywhere, windowsills, tables. It gave everything a nice, mellow ambience. Mona, a tiny woman dressed in a flowing floral dress, greeted them at the door and led them into the dining room where people sat having their cards read, or drinking loose leaf tea. There was the sound of laughter. Everyone seemed to be enjoying themselves. As Tempest observed the room, she was very aware that Mona was observing her. "You must be Tempest," she stated rather coldly, "thank you for coming."

"You're welcome."

Mona looked up at Paul and smiled radiantly. "Lots of people want cold readings, and cards. So many asked for you to read their cards. Tempest can do the cold readings."

Tempest shook her head slowly. She wants Paul. How easy it was to read Mona, her thought processes transparent, like looking through glass. She wanted Paul, and resented her presence. Well that was too

bad. As Mona pulled Paul along to one of the tables, talking all the way, she entered the party, and simply basked in the atmosphere. When she saw an empty recliner near the window, she sat and waited. Soon, a shy looking man in jeans and Celtics logo sweatshirt began to stare at her. The energy felt good, and she smiled at him and urged him over to her. When he approached, she was assailed with very strong images. "Would you like a reading?"

" Yes! I wondered if you were one of the psychics."

" I see an elderly woman,..late 70's or early 80's,..name of,..Hilda,..Helga..."

The man opened his mouth to speak, but she shook her head no. " She has shoulder length white hair,..very soft. A very sweet woman."

The man nodded,..his eyes wet.

"Don't worry about her upcoming heart surgery. Two valves will be repaired, and she will heal quickly. Don't worry about her. All will come out fine."

He breathed deeply. "That was amazing. It's my grandmother,Helga. Thank you."

Feeling a pull from her right, Tempest turned to see Paul watching her from the doorway, his expression unreadable. Others approached her, after being told of how accurate she was, and she began to give them readings,..relaxing more with each one.

Paul shook his head, incredulous. Maggie had said she was good, but this good? She was something to see in action, no hesitation or doubt as she told you her vision. Impressive.

Mona came up and grabbed his arm, breaking his concentration. "Why haven't you called me? You promised to take me out again, and I never took you for a liar."

Paul chuckled. " I never promised to go out again. What are you talking about?"

"Read me. Tell me what I feel." Mona gazed up at him expectantly,hungrily.

Paul almost laughed aloud, she looked so ready for a passionate kiss. Gently removing her arm, he rejoined his table, not bothering to accept her challenge. Psychic groupies...ugh.

"I'm exhausted." Tempest felt drained. She lay back against the headrest, reclined her seat, and closed her eyes. Lips gently touched hers, retreated. It was a tender, friendly kiss, not at all passionate. "You take advantage of me, Paul."

"Couldn't help it. You look so kissable right now."

Opening her eyes, she smiled, not offended. "Is it normal to feel so tired and empty after one of these parties?"

"It usually is draining. You'll learn to shield yourself better the more you do them." After a moment, he added, "Maybe you should skip the Brookline party. You won't be missing anything."

Tempest sat forward. "I have to meet this Michael. It's important because I might know him."

"How?"

"He showed up for a reading."

Pauls shock was obvious. "At Maggie's? I doubt that. He's gifted himself."

"Alright..but how does he use it?"

"Well what kind of question is this?"

"Nothing, forget it. I just need to meet him."

They drove the rest of the way in silence. When they reached the shop he parked, and turned to face her." When he came to you, what happened? What did he want?"

"I don't know. He left fast. I can't understand my reaction to him, it was unlike anything I've picked up before."

"Was it a good feeling?"

"Yes..but it changed. No, not good at all."

Paul sighed, before opening her door. "Tempest,..watch out with him. He's a strange one, and not of the light."

"Not of the light?"

"I repeat,..not of the light."

As they got out of the car, Tempest glanced at her watch. It was 9:00, exactly the time stated on the invitation. Situated on a side street, it's red canopy like others near it, Odds and Ends Oddity Shop would have been difficult to find.

Before going in, she peered through the window. A flawless crystal ball sat there on a pedestal of six silver dragons, their emerald eyes glowing. There were several urns of various shapes and hue, and some sort of skull, polished to a rich gloss.

Paul opened the door for her to enter. There were three steps leading up to the shop. Several women were visible, dressed in black or silver. A few men stood behind a counter. The air smelled of ,..what? A rich, musky scent hard to identify.

Paul took her arm protectively, and she didn't object. Eyes turned to them, interested, curious, even a bit hostile. And then Michael appeared.

He entered from a back room, a young blonde clinging to his arm. He wore a loose black cotton shirt and black jeans, and Tempest was struck by how handsome he was. His pale hair was still in a ponytail, and she knew it was he who'd come to her office. No more doubt. His gaze swept the room, then settled on her.

Pauls grip tightened on her arm. " You need to get out of here."
"Not yet."

She crossed the room to approach him, and Paul followed. When she reached Michael, he pushed the blonde away. " Hello Tempest. Feeling better?" This time his voice was the smoothest cognac, resonant, clear. She stepped closer. The arousal was immediate. It gripped her abdomen, an almost painful tension. Her chest tightened and she felt as if she was encased in an aggressive hug. She could almost feel him within her, and her body responded. Embarrassed, she averted her eyes.

Michael touched her chin with one finger, lifting her face, drawing her eyes to his. The effect couldn't have been more disorienting. Stumbling, she grabbed his arm and he steadied her, whispering in her ear, "It's alright. Control it. You'll feel better shortly,..and then we need to talk."

Tempest stood there feeling as if she'd just had the most intense sex of her life. As her pulse steadied, she looked back at Paul.

He was horrified. The look he gave her was so full of concern and a sort of fear, that she felt ashamed.

"We're getting out of here,..now." He reached for her but she pulled back. Feeling completely out of control,..well, she didn't like it. She needed answers.

"No Paul..please. I need to talk to him,..to figure out what is going on."

"Why? Don't you know that you've just been raped? Let's go!"

Stunned, she blurted,"Wha...what do you mean? He didn't even touch me."

"Oh?" Paul was in a rage, his dark eyes fierce." He raped you.

Believe me about this. You have to leave!"

Tempest thought about it. She would admit that something had happened...but rape? That was ridiculous. She looked at the nervous way Paul watched the others, the anger in his stance. "Why do you hate him?"

Paul visibly sagged. "You are so naive. Can't you trust me about this? I've been doing this longer than you. I know certain things, and you need to get out of here."

" She can't." Michael took her hand in his fluidly, as if it belonged there. He seemed to appear from nowhere. " I invited her and she is my guest. You, on the other hand, are...an intruder."

"I invited him." Tempest struggled to get the words out, feeling strangely lethargic.

Paul watched her, fragile in her loose fitting dress, her hair slightly disheveled around her face. She was flushed, her eyes bright. The young blonde who'd been with Michael earlier came and led her away.

Focusing completely on Paul, Michael sneered, " I want this woman, and I will have her. She is perfect. A natural empath and healer, a powerful one born to it. Never have I encountered someone with such promise. But you know all of this already,..don't you Paul?"

Paul felt Michael's malice in waves, battering at him, but he withstood it. True, he was no match for the man before him, but Tempest deserved a choice. "You overlook one thing Michael. She has chosen the path of light."

Michael chuckled and nodded. "Do your teachings not say that woman is mans wisdom? Allow her to be mine."

"But you allow her nothing! She is like a child and..."

"Enough. Leave her in the hands of your God ....and get out, now. I won't be denied."

Paul cringed, knowing instinctively that he was no match for Michael,..not now. He would be a fool to challenge him. He looked around for her...to try to call her to him, but somehow, she was hidden from view. Damn! Frustrated,he shook his head. "Why hide her from me. Afraid she will go?"

Chuckling, Michael smiled at him. "Just leave. I'm not one to take chances, and you lost yours,..obviously."

Frustrated, and not sure what to do, Paul left, slamming the door behind him.

CHAPTER FIVE

Tempest saw Paul leave. Alarmed, she tried to go after him, but several people began to talk to her, seemingly to draw her attention away from him. Excusing herself, she quickly walked toward the exit.

Michael intercepted her and grasped her elbow. "Your friend had to leave unexpectedly. I told him that I would see you home." He began to guide her back to the others.

Something was terribly wrong. She knew Paul wouldn't desert her. He was probably upset that she didn't listen to him, but he wouldn't leave her. But try as she would, she couldn't read Michael.

The attraction was still there, now a gentle pulse, and the complete absence of the revulsion she'd felt at their first meeting...it didn't make sense.

Tempest stared at the exit stairs, her escape, wishing Paul would appear, but he was really gone. A tall glass of wine was pressed into her hand by a customer. Paul, what made you abandon me? She felt disoriented, as if the room was growing dim, all light filtering through a veil of dark gauze.

Michael's voice reached her, soft and sensual, " Tempest,..you have to learn to focus and direct your perceptions. If you don't, each new revelation will carry you where it may. Don't you hate the confusion?"

Unnerved, she looked up at him. Seldom could someone read her so well. Paul,..he'd said she was raped. Was that accurate?

" No. Paul is a wanna be, a fledgling. There is so much he doesn't understand. His reaction was one of jealousy, that's all."

Chilled, Tempest sipped her wine. Had she spoken aloud,..or was he reading her mind? Michael was leading her towards the room she noticed earlier, in the rear of the shop. Planting herself, she resisted his gentle lead. He stopped and gave her a dazzling smile. "What is it?"

She shook her head slightly, trying to clear it, but the muffled sound of conversations and whispers cluttered her mind, making it impossible to concentrate. The aroma in the air was thick, almost suffocating.

" Tempest,..are you ill?"

" I have to go. could you call me a cab?"

" Why, what's wrong?" Michael focused his beautifully vivid eyes on her and the blood rushed to her head.

Fighting it, she tore her gaze away, almost immediatly feeling better. "How do you know me? Who told you about me?"

" My poor Tempest. You were a revelation to me. The source doesn't matter. I can be a revelation to you also,..if you let me. Don't you want to know all that you're capable of? When the other kids shunned you for seeing too much, or chased you and threw rocks at your house, calling you a witch,..didn't you promise yourself you'd find out the truth?"

Tempest felt the first real beginning of fear. He knew too much!

"What about when your father beat you harshly at age seven..wasn't it? Telling you to keep your mouth shut, keep it to yourself. Didn't you cry that you'd understand it all one day?"

Horrible! It was horrible to have this stranger know her life, to walk into her memories uninvited. "Who the hell are you!"

He smiled at her almost lovingly, but not quite. "I am the answer to your questions. Come with me."

She let him lead her into the back room and was surprised to find herself standing in a cheerful white and yellow kitchen. Through the kitchen was an archway, and beyond that stairs leading upward. It was dark there, and she was reminded of a hidden, dank cave. The smell of mold filled her nostrils, then quickly faded, along with the imagery. It was just an archway, and stairs. I'm in trouble, she realized at last. Oh Paul, i'm in such trouble. Why didn't I trust you? Come back! And the arousal was returning, a tense anticipation at her very core. Sensitivity to Michael's every move. She attempted to retreat to the shop but he held her hand, as if waiting. Silent. "Michael...I can't do this."

Encircling her in his arms, he pulled her close and pressed his lips to hers. The effect was startling, melting the last of her reservations. He probed her lips with his tongue and she willingly parted them to meet his tongue with her own. Her emotions had control of her now,..she was lost.
Michael lifted her in his arms, crossed the kitchen, and ascended the stairs.

Paul sat in his car and punched the steering wheel. A small beep erupted, his horn. He couldn't remember ever being this frustrated. He genuinely liked Tempest, was attracted to her, yet he'd left her in danger. It traced his spine, a sense of danger. Michael! He'd knew many things about the man, and one theme often repeated was that he was master of the dark arts,...and to never cross him. He was a powerful man, no denying it, and poor Tempest had caught his attention. The man had some use for her. Men like Michael didn't fall in love. Hell, men like himself rarely did. But there was something about Tempest, an honesty and sweetness. Paul had felt her arousal, her climax, while her eyes were glued to that mans eyes, and it angered him. How could she fight someone that strong, that skilled? She was a lamb ripe for slaughter! There had to be something he could do.

A small voice whispered within, "not tonight. She's on her own tonight." Paul slipped the car into drive, feeling deeply depressed, for he'd learned to trust his small voice. She truly was on her own...seemed the universe ordained it.

*   *   *

Michael carried Tempest into a bedroom, his bedroom. It was huge, and entirely black. Black walls, black carpet, black laquered four poster bed, and dressers. Esquisitely designed black caste iron sconces on each wall with lit candles. The only other illumination was from the full moon visible through a huge picture window. He gently slid her down his body to stand in his embrace. "This is inevitable you know," he stated softly before kissing her forehead. "Why fight it?"

His voice was soothing to her soul. Tempest relaxed against him. Michael caressed her neck, the small of her back. "We are of the spirit, you and I. There is more in store for us than the telling of fortunes."

She sighed as he unzipped the back of her dress, letting it slip from her body to puddle at her feet. Tempest surrendered to all the emotions consuming her. "We have a destiny," he whispered, kissing the curve of her neck.

I'm in a movie, she thought, and i'm about to be devoured.
A tiny thing within her struggled once more to stop this. To bring to a halt what felt like a roller coaster ride. But when she reached out to deter him, her hands encountered bare flesh. He was nude. Folding her against him, almost painfully, he let her know there was no turning back. Once more she was lifted in his arms, carried to the bed. Roughly, she pulled the band from his ponytail, releasing his hair which cascaded to his shoulders like molten gold. She kissed it, so cool to her lips.

Together they fell across the bed, him atop her, but catching his weight with his arms. Tempest looked up into his eyes, drowned in them as the irises seemed to expand. "You are mine," he growled before dropping his weight upon her. And lord help her, she was. Completely.

As the beginning of dawn filled the window, its golden haze invading the darkness, she finally fell into a deep sleep.
Michael watched her sleep. He brushed her hair from her face. Then he rose and stared down at her nude body. "Beautiful", he mused, then covered her with the cool silk sheet. She curled into a fetal position. He

smiled, feral in the dim light. Donning a red robe, he left her, closing the door.

CHAPTER SIX

Waking spoon fashion against Michael's back, Tempest was assaulted by the urge to vomit. Although the room was radiant with early morning light, she was enveloped in a vapor of darkness, and foul odor. Gagging, she sat up, trying to breathe. No, it couldn't be Michael, not now. Not after last night! Tears gathered behind her eyes, but gradually the feelings began to fade. Her stomach calmed, then the cloud of evil thinned, until only the sunshine remained.

Michael rolled over on his side to grin at her. "Are you alright?"

She nodded, trying to understand what it was about him. What was this pull, and revulsion, at the same time. How could she have fallen into bed with this man she barely knew?

He rubbed her arm. "You looked really ill for a moment there."

"I'm okay now Michael. But for a while, well, never mind."

He pulled her back on the bed, kissing her passionately. "I hope you're not angry I didn't take you home. You were sleeping so good, and..."

"No, it's okay. I just think I should get my car now and head home."

Michael got up and walked nude to the dresser, without a hint of embarrassment. Lifting a key, he admitted," Your car is outside. I got it while you slept."

" You went in my bag?"

"Yes. Don't be modest. I've been in things more personal than your bag."

Tempest wasn't ready for playful banter. She didn't want to take a shower, or eat breakfast and spend any more time with this man. Instead, she felt ashamed and totally out of her element. Locating her dress and underwear folded on the end of the bed, she quickly dressed.

Leaning back against the dresser, and crossing his legs, comfortable as could be in his handsome nudity, Michael asked, "Why are you rushing off,..or should I say, running away?"

" I don't understand what's happening to me. You have to give me time to absorb all of this..."

He came over and buttoned the back of her dress. "Tempest. What happened will not go away. Our destiny will not go away. You will be back,..and i'll wait. But I won't wait too long."

Seeing the way the sunlight reflected off his hair, like a halo, she tenderly rubbed a hunk of it between her fingers.

"You're probably right. But inside, I feel I should be alone,..to figure this out. I don't really believe in destiny. I believe in choices."

Taking her face in his hands, he kissed her deeply, taking her breath away, skillfully awakening her senses, then stepping away he whispered," The only choice is whether to accept your destiny and make life easy, or fight that destiny, and make life,..difficult."

Trembling, she retrieved her bag from the dresser. She remembered how he'd claimed her that night, and proclaimed her his. How his touch had consumed her. Tempest rushed to the door, and raced down the stairs, desperate to put distance between them before she began to crave him again!

When she entered the kitchen there were two women seated at the table. The young blonde from the party, and an older, dark haired woman. They grinned at her knowingly, and she grew warm with embarrassment. Nodding a greeting at them, she entered the shop, where a few customers browsed. Once outside she breathed the polluted hair, and thought it the sweetest air she'd ever smelled.

Her car was parked right in front of the shop. As she got in and put it in drive, her muscles protested and she remembered her night with Michael, vividly. The man had posessed her, bringing her to a threshold of pleasure she never thought possible. But there was something almost cruel and harsh in his posession. He felt like a hunter, and she felt like,..prey.

Tempest's thoughts turned to Paul as she pulled into traffic and headed home. What must he think of her? She needed to talk to him on Monday, to try to explain what was happening to her. What was real after all, the intense attraction for Michael's mind and body, or the occasional foul emanations. Which was the true Man? One person who might be able to tell her was Paul.

CHAPTER SEVEN

Paul paced in the front lobby, glanced up at the clock, then paced some more. He held two books under one arm.

Maggie watched him curiously from her desk, but said nothing. Paul was the most laid back person she knew. So, seeing him in this aggitated state amazed her. She opened her mouth to ask why he was so upset, but changed her mind.

When Tempest came in, he froze, staring at her. Before she could greet him, he grabbed her arm and pulled her to his office. When he closed the door behind them, he blurted,"Tell me what happened? Couldn't you see you were in danger?"

Tempest stiffened. She had come to work with every intention of telling Paul that she was sorry. That maybe he'd been right, and she should have left with him. And to try to make him understand how she felt about Michael. But now that he was talking to her this way,as if she was stupid,..well, she was no longer inclined to tell him anything!

Taking a deep breath, Paul spoke again, much calmer. "I'm sorry I left you the other night. I should'nt have left you. At the time, I thought I should,..but I can't forgive myself for it. There is no way you could protect yourself from him." He sat at his desk, deposited the books there, and leaning back in his chair, closed his eyes. "You slept with him." It wasn't a question. His expression revealed his disappointment.

Tempest wasn't sure what to say. Paul looked so angry, and something more. "I think I love him Paul. Just being near him drives me crazy. I can't get him out of my head. All day Sunday, I tried..but its like I'm drawn to him. The bad things I used to feel around him have faded almost completely away."

"He's not for you!"

"What are you talking about? He knows me better than anyone else. I admit, he's cocky and arrogant, demanding. But you act as if he's a mass murderer, who will kill me. He had a chance, and all he did was love me."

"love you, huh?" Paul grinned mirthlessly. " Men like him don't love. He needs you. I have my ideas why. He may not murder you, but he'll kill you just the same. He's more than you think. Not just a psychic,..he's..."

" What!? He's what? Why won't you tell me what you know about him, instead of speaking in riddles? Can you make me stop needing him?"

"Dammit Tempest! You don't need him. You barely know him, so how can you love him? But he knows everything you need, your every desire. He may give them to you, but you'll pay dearly."

Tempest shook her head. This sounded crazy. Deep inside, she knew Paul made sense, but what she felt for Michael was so strong! "Please, just stop Paul. I can't deal with all of this."

"You damn well better deal with it. I'm talking about your life. There's alot you haven't heard of. There really are dark practices, and that's what he specializes in. I can't believe that you are so desperate to learn, you'll only see what you want to see. Open your eyes".

Tempest started to see his logic, but then she remembered her night with Michael, the way he held her, his mouth on her skin, the way he possessed her body with his. " I wouldn't do anything evil, not for anyone. He's just a man. Maybe I can help him learn to do good. Did you think of that?"

Paul almost grabbed Tempest, to shake some sense into her.There had to be something he could do to convince her. Wait.."You can read me Tempest. I'm open. Am I lying to you?"

She focused on him,..allowed herself to feel him. "Well, no."

"Am I crazy?"

"Of course not."

"And tell me. What do I think of you?"

Tempest felt herself encased in warmth and peace. "You like me very much."

"Yes, I do. So please, do something for me." Paul picked up the books, walked over and handed them to her. "These were written by a man named Tabor Ashe. He owned the shop before Michael, and he also was Michaels' teacher, about the arts. Read them. Try to be open to the workings of his mind.

You just might realize more from them, than Michael would ever reveal."

She wanted to hug him because he was so worried about her, but instead, she simply took the books. They were very heavy, the bindings frayed with age. "Where is this Tabor Ashe now?"

Paul stared at her, his gaze colder than she'd ever seen it. "He's dead. Found mutilated and tortured four years ago."

A chill passed through her.

Paul held her shoulders, and earnestly stated," I'm here Tempest. Remember that, no matter what. I'll only let you play with this fire a little while,...then I'm gonna end this game. Understand?"

An image tried to form, shifting mass and color behind her eyes, but before it could take shape, Tempest turned and fled his office. His parting words rang in her head. That wasn't the Paul she knew.

By the end of the day, Tempest had to see Michael. His essence filled her senses. She could almost feel his touch. Images danced through her mind of the night they spent together, and she could hear his soothing voice.

The books were locked in her desk. Paul was concerned, but he didn't need to be so afraid for her. She'd always been able to take care of herself, so why should this be any different. She couldn't even contemplate not going to Michael. He was a magnet to her.

Locking her office, she walked to the front door, anxious to see him again. Just as she reached the door, Maggie called out to her. Tempest hated being delayed, but walked over to her desk instead. " Hi Maggie."

"Hi dear. I meant to ask you how you liked Mona's party saturday?"

"It was really nice. I enjoyed it."

"Well, you see, Mona asked that I don't send you to any further parties she arranges, and I don't understand. All your clients rave about your accuracy. Did something happen?"

Tempest smiled at her. The curiosity was killing Maggie. Well, she could satisfy that. "Mona doesn't want me around Paul. She wants him, and thinks he wants me."

"And are you and Paul seeing each other?"

"Maggie, we're good friends. That's all."

Maggie nodded. "Have a good night then, Tempest."

As she walked out the door, she called out, "I'll try."

CHAPTER EIGHT

Tempest pulled up in front of Odds and Ends,and parked. It was very quiet. A few people walked toward the bus stop at the corner,but otherwise,the street was empty. It smelled like it might rain, crisp and salty. She looked at the shop, and saw that all the windows were dark. There wasn't a hint of movement inside. She got out and gazed at the upstairs windows. There was slight illumination in one of them, and she wondered if it was Michael's bedroom. He appeared in the window as if on cue, to look down at her. By the time she reached the door, he was pulling it open. Dragging her inside, he pulled her close, kissing her.

There was a rightness in the way her body fit against his, the manner in which he kissed her. A sense of being where she belonged. Paul had to be wrong! Michael held out to her that one thing she desired most, knowledge of all she could be. Why should she deny herself such happiness, love and meaning?

She couldn't.

Leading her to the kitchen, he smiled happily. "I closed the shop early tonight, hoping you would come."

She sat at the table while he made fragrant coffee, relaxing from the long day. They were like any normal couple, she mused, nothing strange about them. He handed her a cup, and asked nonchalantly,"So,..what did Paul say to you today?"

Tempest put her cup down, trying to think of a way to avoid this conversation.

"I know he begged you to stay away from me, right? You see, even though he doesn't know it yet, he's in love with you." Carrying his own coffee, he sat next to her at the table. "So please tell me what lies he told you, attempting to keep you away from me?"

She started to reply, but stopped when he warned,"I'll know if you're lying."

What should she do? Telling the truth would only make things worse between these two men. It would be like betraying Paul,in a way. Why couldn't Michael just drop it? She was here with him, wasn't she? "Nothing important, just forget it."
He stiffened, and fixed her with his gaze. She tried to look away, but failed miserably. That gaze was like a magnet.

"Sweetie, tell me what he said, and let me be the judge of its worth."

"Michael,..you know how he feels. Why ask me?"

"I need you to tell me, or do you have something to hide?"

"Hide,.. from you? Don't be ridiculous." Her heart quickened when she noticed a tightening of his jaw and mouth. "He thinks you're dangerous." Immediatly, she felt guilty.

"Dangerous? How?"

"Is it true, do you study the black arts? Is that what you intend for me to do? Because I won't."

Michael didn't laugh or smile. In fact he looked angry,no,seething. "Your friend has strange ideas about me. Perhaps I need to set him straight.Can't have him thinking I'll abuse you in any way."

Something in his voice panicked her, and she touched his hand. It felt cold. "I talked to him and its alright now. He was just looking out for me. No need to get angry about it."

"Looking out for you is my job now."

Michael's look froze her blood. His blue eyes had grown hard as glass. There was something cunning in his face, and at once she became worried for Paul. "Please, promise me you'll let this thing with Paul go. I don't want bad blood between the two of you."

He drank his coffee, not replying either way.

"Please? He's a good friend. Drop this."

"No. I won't. He needs to understand that he has no place in this. None."

" He's a friend. So he does in a way." She hated to argue with him, but had the distinct feeling that Paul was now in danger. The idea of him being hurt terrified her.

"Michael, don't do anything..please? I won't be able to forgive you for it."

He finally relaxed, although a frown still creased his handsome face. "I can't have you angry at me, can I?"

Tempest finished her coffee, unable to truly relax until he was smiling again. Then she realized they had the whole place to themselves, and the quiet was welcome. Maybe she'd succeeded in averting a disaster.

"Come with me," he urged, pulling her to her feet. She followed him into the shop. "I have something for you." From behind the counter he produced a large obsidian globe.It sat on a flawless circle of silver. "Circles will work good with you, because of your native blood. No beginning, no end, a simple concept of your culture. This ball will be useful in your concentration excercises. Would you like to try one now?"

Excitement exploded within her. Nodding, she rubbed her hands around the smooth globe. How beautiful it was, and so cool to the touch.

Placing his hand over hers, Michael whispered,"Close your eyes. Really feel it's texture. Probe it. Look for any imperfections. Focus solely on the globe and its diameters,..nothing else."

She tried, but his hand on hers was distracting. Gently removing his hand, she closed her eyes, thinking of the cool substance beneath her fingers. She grew aware of the ticking of a nearby clock, and a bush softly hitting a window. Refocusing her thoughts, she concentrated on the obsidian.

Dark, hard, solid. It's density resisted her mental probe. She began to surrender in defeat.

"Try again,"he whispered, close to her ear, but her body only became hyper aware of his body behind her. She obeyed, moving her hand around the globe. There were no chips or dents. Looking deeply into it, she noticed that there was one small area lighter than the rest. Imagining that her thoughts were sharp, piercing...she channeled that image into the sphere, battering at the resistance until suddenly, there wasn't any. Just air and clarity. Puzzled, she shook her head, clearing it.

"Funny, but at first there was a lot of resistance. Then, it was like an opening,.. all clear."

Michael hugged her. "Good! There is an air bubble in the very center of this globe. I didn't expect you to find it so quickly!"

His excitement was catching. Tempest kissed the globe and grinned up at him. ed., proud of herself. He gave her a look that stripped her bare inside. "What is it?"

"I see far,little one. But perhaps not far enough."

"What exactly do you see for us?" She wrapped her arms around his waist and pressed her cheek to his chest, listening to the steady beat of his heart. With anyone else she would get fleeting images or thoughts, being this close. With him, she felt nothing at all. As if she stood in a vacuum. She couldn't read him at all.

" I see you living here with me, with perfect understanding. I have so much to show and teach you. And you can teach me things too. How does that sound?" He kissed the top of her head.

Pulling away slightly, she admitted." I can't see anything about you, Michael. I can't read you at all. Nothing comes through. That kind of scares me."

"Don't be afraid of me. I only have your best interests at heart."

"Not your own?"

"Okay, you got me. My own interest too. But then again,..you are my interests."

"Explain that to me." A chill inched its way into Tempest's heart, closing it a little.

Michael took the ball from her hands, and she thought it glowed with a hidden fire. When he looked at her again, his eyes glowed with the same flame. A fierceness. " I see what you will become Tempest. When the clay you are now is molded, forged, and strengthened by fire, you promise to be so...unique. I want you, and I hope I deserve you."

Lowering her eyes, she tried to digest all he'd said. This night,..hell, the entire day. Something nagged at her. you want me, but do you love me.

You even said Paul loves me..but you never said you do.

CHAPTER NINE

Paul sat deep in his recliner rolling two polished silver balls in his hands. They produced a soft tinkling of bells as they rotated in his palms. Usually they relaxed him, but not tonight.

He replayed his conversation with Tempest in his mind. He remembered the look of incredulity on her face, and a hint of fear. He was so frustrated with her! She was no match for Michael, and he'd easily seduced her. What was it Tabor Ashe had written? Focus your intentions upon the desired person, and achieve true affection for them. In this way you will easily understand them, and be able to please them. Was that what Michael had done? Focused his mind on Tempest, studied her, and pleased her?

Well he had certainly taken control and focused on her the night of the party. His intensity was visible as a bright, grayish aura. So much power in one so young, so much negativity.

How quickly Tempest had succumbed to his manipulation. The very things he liked about her, honesty, sincerity, and being naive. Her child like ways,were being used against her. She saw these things in Michael, but he was only showing her a reflection of herself. The little puppet was foolish enough to believe she was in control. What was the best way to protect her?

All of his meditation and prayer only clarified the problem he faced. He wanted Tempest for himself,..that had been a true revelation. Michael now had Tempest. If he wanted to take her from his dark clutches,..he'd have to fight Michael himself. To do that he'd have to begin to trust in himself again, and overcome the many years of docile existence. Most of all, he'd have to trust the Creator who made him. Paul finally realized he was free to face the problem he'd always struggled to overcome. Doubt. Doubt that the Creator approved of, and loved him.

"She needs me," he whispered, dropping the silver orbs to the mahogany carpet where they rolled and tinkled until coming to rest against the black leather couch. "She needs me so much!"

Tempest ran her finger down the long curve of Michaels spine to the spot where it vanished beneath the sheets. Sighing, he turned to pull her into his arms. Snuggling against his chest, she languished there, feeling the warmth of his breath on her face. She was overjoyed that no foulness wafted off of him this time. Softly, she said," You didn't let me finish my story."

He rubbed his face in her hair, kissed it. "I know. You have a way of distracting me." He rubbed his leg between hers lazily.

Moving to draw his leg closer, she whispered, " Will you let me finish it now?"

"No". Laughing softly, he rolled her beneath him. "Because nothing you tell me explains why you can't move in with me now. They're both dead, and you live all alone." He touched a particulary sensitive spot, making her gasp.

"No fair, Michael. How can I make a decision when....?"

He kissed her deeply, his hands caressing her. Then grinning down at her he teased, "Who said I play fair?"

"It's still too soon for me to move in. You...have to....wait a while."

The time for words ended as he kissed her again.

Laying on her side, Tempest took deep breaths until her respiration was almost normal again. Michael was watching her, his look an intimate caress. Strangely, she thought of Paul.

Making love to Michael was intense, exhausting. What would it be like to make love to Paul? She imagined he'd be slow, gentle..thorough. Just as consuming in his mature way. Almost spiritual.

The bed bounced as Michael got up. He dressed quickly, a scowl on his face.

"Where are you going? I told you I'd quit the shop, and I did." Something about his movements alarmed her.

"I'll bring back Chinese." Just like that, he was gone.

Paul locked his office door and walked to the front desk where Maggie browsed through a magazine.

"She really quit?"

Startled, she dropped the magazine and stifled a screech.

"Yeah, she called me today. Tempest is moving on. She was good too."

"Do you know where she works days?"

"Some medical office on Joy Street, near the state house. Why?"

He forced a grin on his face. "It's real important that I see her."

Maggie grinned like a cat with fresh cream. "Paul! You have a thing for miss priss. She's a strange one."

"She's a nice person Maggie."

"Umm...well she said she'd be in this week to get some things from her office, and pay the final rent on the office."

Just then the door slammed open and Michael burst in. Ignoring Maggie, he walked up to Paul. "Good. Just who I want to see. We need to talk."

Chilled, Maggie locked her desk. "um, sir..do you have an appointment?"

"I said that Paul and I need to talk." Michael fixed a threatening look on her. "Maggie, isn't it? Mind your business and shut up." She whimpered. He looked like he wanted to kill her.

Paul snapped, "You're here for me. Leave her alone!" He headed for his office and Michael followed.

Sitting on his desk, Paul lit a cigarette and smiled after inhaling deeply. "So, what's up homey? Got a beef with me?"

"Yes. Her name is Tempest."

"Ah yes. Tempest. So what are your plans for our Tempest?"

Michael's eyes became slits. "You don't want to tangle with me. Life promises to be good for you, as long as you back off."

"Oh well. Tough shit on me I guess, 'cause i'm not backing off. That woman deserves better than your plans for her."

"Paul, I promise you. You are no match for me. She doesn't want you hurt, but I...it makes no difference to me."

Feeling his malice, Paul felt slightly nauseous. So thats what Tempest had experienced. "I'm so afraid. Listen, you malignant son of a bitch, don't threaten me. Don't underestimate me, you might be surprised."

Standing his full height, Michael sneered, "I know what you are!"

Still seated and calm, Paul grinned at him. "And I know what you are. What about it? That woman is special, and i'll be damned if you destroy her."

Michael laughed mirthlessly. "I know what kind of special she is. You just want her in your bed. You want her tongue deep in your mouth, to feel her soft skin. All the pleasures that are already mine!"

"She's yours, huh? Then why the hell are you here? Threatened by me maybe? Looks like your job's cut out for you homey. May the best man win."

Michael balled his fists at his sides. So softly that Paul barely heard him, he whispered, "He will. count on it."

When Michael left his office, Paul took a deep breath to steady himself. Well, you are really in it now, he thought.
A feeling of excitement filled him. He actually wanted to laugh. It had been a long time since he'd felt excited.

Maggie raced into his office. "You alright?"

Smiling at her, he stood up and said, "Never felt better. C'mon. I'll help you lock up and walk you to your car."

Maggie looked up at him worriedly. "This is about Tempest isn't it?" Paul actually laughed. He felt good. "C'mon. lets get out of here."

CHAPTER TEN

Maggie chattered nervously all the way to her car. First about Mona's party, then about Tempest. "You know what? Six people called Monday morning, to arrange readings with Tempest. Her reputation spread since Mona's party. Too bad she left us."

Paul just nodded, and watched her get safely into her car, and lock the doors. When she finally pulled away he was flooded with relief. From now on he didn't know what to expect. Being with him probably wasn't the safest place to be.

Getting into his Nissan, he secured his seatbelt before pulling into traffic. It was thicker than usual, due to an event happening in the Commons, some sort of free concert. He was starved and decided to stop before going home, to get something to eat. Pizza seemed good. He kept his eyes peeled for the local pizzaria, heading for the familiar turf of the North End. Just as he exited the off ramp from the highway and gently touched the brakes, there was a loud bang, and his car listed to the right, making him lose control. The Nissan crossed the dividing line although he struggled with the wheel, gently braking. A large truck was bearing down on him, beeping its horn frantically.

With all of his strength, Paul wrenched the wheel toward the correct lane, pleased as his car responded and swerved to the left, avoiding the truck which whizzed past. Pulling off to the side of the road, he waited for his racing heart and pulse to calm. Paul got out of his car, and after inspecting it, realized the left front wheel was flat. Upon closer scrutiny, a large tear was visible. His inner voice tried to speak, but ignoring it, he changed the tire. Then, his appetite gone, Paul drove home.

When he pulled onto his street, he saw flashing red lights, and fire engines right in front of his building! Parking, he jumped out of his car and ran the distance to see smoke pouring from the top floor, where his apartment was located.

All of his belongings, some too important to lose,..up there. He asked a fireman holding a hose what happened. "Not sure. No one goes up there until we know it's safe."

Crossing the street, Paul stood with his neighbors and hoped for the best. His mind was reeling. Can all of this be a coincidence? The flat tire almost cost him his life, and now this. The small voice within finally broke free. You know this is Michael's doing. He fights dirty.

Alerted, he looked up and down the street. Was there someone further down, near his car? Just as he decided to go investigate, someone tugged at his shoulder. It was an older man who lived in his building. "I wouldn't worry too much. Doubt there's any real damage. Some kid playing with matches set some papers on fire in his kitchen."

Paul managed a smile. "I hope you're right." Stealing a glance toward his car,..he saw no one was there now. Had he imagined it? He doubted that. The firetrucks began to pull away, and they were told it was safe to go in.

The hallway was soaked because of the sprinkler system, and trampled wet plaster littered the worn carpet, but by a miracle, his apartment was intact. The only problem was the heavy odor of smoke. He opened all of the windows to let the night air dispense the odors. What a day!

Collapsing on his soft leather couch, Paul thought about all that had transpired. Michael wasn't wasting any time. But he wasn't about to back off. He'd taken the step over the line now, and was destined to walk the road to the bitter end.

*   *   *

Tempest sat at the kitchen table, studying the obsidian globe. Waiting, for what she didn't know. She was so immersed, that she didn't hear anyone enter until they stood in the room with her. It was the young blonde from the party. The girls eyes were wide with surprise.

"Where's Michael?"

Surprised herself, and suspicious, Tempest sat up in her chair. "He's out. Care to wait for him?"

"What are you doing here?"

Studying the girl, Tempest decided she couldn't be a day over seventeen. She was slender as a willow, and fresh like the California types in the movies. Receiving clear images from the girl, she grew worried. This wasn't good at all. The girl was bonded to Michael, and saw her as an intruder. The girl actually felt she belonged to him!

Tempest didn't feel jealous, and wondered about that. Shouldn't she feel some jealousy? "I remember you. Gloria, right...or should I say glory?"

The girls eyes clouded. "You call me Gloria. You didn't answer my question. Why are you here?!"

She wasn't sure how to answer. Gloria was hurting, and hateful right now. Nothing she had to say would make things any better. Finally, Tempest simply told the truth.

"I'll be here alot from now on, Gloria." Taking a deep breath, she asked, "Are you with Michael? Have I stepped in when I shouldn't have?"

Tears fell from Glorias eyes. "I hate you," she sniffled. "You're a bitch, just as evil as he is!"

Tempest was stunned, and listened to the girls tirade with disbelief.

"Now that you're here it's ruined. You won't share him. I can tell!"

"Share him,..you mean Michael?"

"Yes! He belongs to so many of us, and we love him. But you, the great psychic, you want him all to yourself!"

Tempest felt the beginning of both fear, and anger.

Gloria snapped, "You are evil as he is! But he is more than any other man could hope to be." A blank look surfaced on her face.

This time Tempest heard the front door open, and soon Michael appeared, with a bag of chinese food. He focused on Gloria, still, as if feeling every nuance in the room. Almost too calmly, he set the bag on the table.

"Glory,..what did I tell you?" His voice was like an early winter chill. Gloria visibly trembled.

She burst into tears, but they failed to move him. Tempest felt sorry for her. Why should she suffer for saying how she felt, for telling the truth. "Michael..stop it."

Holding his hand up to silence her, he asked once more, "What did I tell you?"

"You said to leave you alone. That you found someone else, that it's all over now."

"And..." He glared at her, a storm in his eyes.

"and that we're just friends now!"

"Yet here you are, spreading lies. Upsetting Tempest. What do you say?"

"I'm sorry Tempest. I was,..I was jealous." Gloria ran, sobbing noisily. The door slammed behind her, echoing.

Tempest was stunned! Her mind raced in all directions. That girl was just a baby. Why was he with her? He talked to her like she was a disobedient child. It was kind of sick! Who were the others she mentioned, who loved him? What had she gotten herself into? She glared at him.

"What?" Michael was totally at ease, removing the food from the bag.

" You were so cruel to her. She loves you. That adoring puppy love."

" So that means I should pretend to care about her?"

" No! "

" Well what's your point?"

" The point is you didn't have to humiliate her."

Michael paused to stare at her. His usually expressive gaze aggravating her. "You are really upset."

"Yes, I am. You destroyed her."

"Glory is a spoiled, and simple girl. She needs directness, not coddling."

Tempest tried to stop herself, but the words spilled out."If she's so simple, why were you with her? Who are the others she spoke of, who love you?"

Expecting him to explode, she sat deeper in her chair.

"I can't be angry at you," he murmured, walking over and caressing her cheek. Then he got plates from the cabinet and began arranging the food, deftly avoiding her question.

"Michael, I can't stay tonight. The office won't tolerate another absence. I have some proposals to write."

"Lie. Tell them you're sick."

"No."

They ate in silence.

CHAPTER ELEVEN

Stepping out into the bright noon sunlight, tipping her face upward to bathe in the heated rays, Tempest made a decision. Now was as good a time as any to go to Maggie's shop and collect her belongings. She didn't feel like going to lunch anyway. It was time to look through Tabor Ashe's books. The last night with Michael had been,..unpleasant. And the girl, Gloria, had been so afraid of him. The most important thing, though she was hesitant to admit it, was that she wanted to see Paul.

Circling the well tended front lawn of the State House, she could smell freshly cut grass. Crossing the street, she entered the Commons, using the wide, steep central stairway made of gray stone. She followed the wide path through tall, well situated trees and scampering squirrels looking for a handout.

Leaving the Commons, Tempest stopped at Park Street Station to buy a hot sausage from a vendor, before continuing to the shop.

When she stepped into the Lobby, she was surprised that Maggie jumped up to greet her. "Can I change your mind Tempest?" She stepped around the desk. "There are so many requests for you. You could make so much money."

"Thanks Maggie..but I just can't. One job is enough for me these days. Besides, you know money was never important. But thank you for letting me work here for a short time."

Tempest froze, unable to tear her eyes away from Maggie. What was she seeing? Michael came here..to see paul! He scared her, and was really angry! Oh no!

"Maggie...where's Paul?"

"Paul? In his office. He's been asking for you."

Tempest walked quickly to her old office and grabbed the books from her desk right away. Packing them into her oversized pocketbook, she left . Next, she knocked at Paul's door.

"Come in." His voice made her smile. How dare Michael bother him!

She stepped in and closed the door behind her. He was sitting at his desk, smoking a cigarette, deep in thought. Without looking up, he put it out. "Hi Tempest."

Sitting down, she smiled at him. "Hi." Around him, everything always felt so clear, so calm. "I have to ask you something. Did Michael come see you?"

He studied her for a while, but just when she began to feel uncomfortable, he looked out the window. "Why?"

"When I was talking to Maggie, I got this flash that he came here angry, to see you, and scared her."

Smiling at her, he shook his head. "Yeah,..he came here all riled up. Nothing to worry about."

It was then that she noticed music softly playing, something with flutes...gentle. She had a strong urge to hug him,..to relax in his calmness. To let go of all the drama that had entered her life. "Paul,I missed you."

He got up, circled his desk and pulled her out of the chair, to hug her. It was a comfortable hug, nothing aggressive in it, and she relaxed against him.

"I'm sorry he bothered you Paul. I'm sorry you got drawn into this."

"I'm not." He squeezed her tight before releasing her.

An idea came to her..from out of the blue. But it was strong. "You do cards right?"

He frowned. "That's my specialty."

"I want you to read my cards."

"No. Don't think that's a good idea."

"Why?"

"You know why. What if I see something pertaining to Michael?"

"I'll deal with it." Giving him a pleading smile, Tempest grabbed his hand. "Please Paul? For some reason I need you to."

He stood a moment, thinking, before finally sitting at his desk. He motioned for her to sit opposite him.

Sitting, she watched him closely. He began to shuffle a regular deck of cards. He then carefully shuffled them into four piles. "Touch any pile, right in the center."

She touched the pile closest to him with her index finger.

Paul picked it up, shuffled it three times, then lay them on the table in an arch. "Pick seven."

Quickly, she picked them. Seeing the doubt in his eyes, she said, "Hey, we can do this. It'll be alright."

Paul took the selected seven cards, warmed them between his hands, and then placed them on the table. When he looked at them closely, his jaw tightened. "Chaos," he whispered.

"What?"

He took a breath and began. "You are at a fork in the road. Both paths can be very good for you, but each is very different. Every card is a heart,which means your emotions are very strong right now, but unfocused. I see deceit from an unexpected source,love from a hidden place, and possibly...a child."

"A child?" Stunned, Tempest stared at the cards. "You must be mistaken!"

"No, i'm not. A child is clearly shown, although i'm not sure how it relates to you."

"But I can't have kids." Ashamed, she got up to leave.

"Hold on,..are you sure about that?"

"Yes, dammit". Her tears fell as she kept her back to him.

Soon she felt his arms around her as he stood behind her. "It's okay Tempest. I told you we shouldn't do this."

She shook her head, ashamed and embarrassed. "No...i'm sorry...I just forget sometimes."

He dropped his arms as she turned to him. "I asked you to do this...and i'm alright now." Wiping her eyes, Tempest sighed. "I was twelve when I found out. I...I never bled. My fallopian tubes never functioned. It's hard to face."

She composed herself, hating the sadness in his face. "It was an interesting reading though."

"Yeah...it was. Did you read the books yet?"

"Not yet."

"Will you?"

She pat her pocketbook. "You have my promise Paul. Now i'd better get back to work."

"Want a ride?"   She gave him a grin, one he found so fragile, and mumbled the walk would do her good.

"Wait,"He handed her one of his business cards. "Keep in touch".

She kissed the card, smiled at him, tucked it in her pocket, and left.

Upon leaving his office, she began to cry again. The cards had played a cruel trick on her, and Paul had been right. She shouldn't have made him read her.

CHAPTER TWELVE

" I don't like you living here alone!" Michael jumped up from her couch to glare at her.

"I'm a big girl,in case you didn't notice!" Tempest stormed through her living room and into the kitchen. Opening a can of Pepsi, she sipped it, trying to calm down. It was so quiet in the living room.

"Michael, what are you doing?" Silence. She stepped back into the living room and found him standing at the window, staring out.

" I don't like arguing with you," he stated, not turning to face her.

"Then stop trying to force me to move in with you. I told you I'm not ready for that yet."

He sighed, those perfect shoulders slumping with the breath. Feeling guilty, she wondered if she was really being difficult. After all, she spent every night with him. He taught her to focus her mind, and once, she'd almost picked up on his thoughts while they made love. But to actually move in,..spending every free moment with him...no, not yet.

"I'm sorry Michael. I just can't leave here and move in with you."

He turned and finally faced her. "You're making this difficult, sweetheart. Eventually, you will move in with me."

She drank her soda thoughtfully. Was the trick in the way he stated everything so positively? Maybe this was the first time his patience had been really tested. Something caught his attention, and following his gaze, she saw it lock on one of the books Paul had given her. She had been reading it when he dropped by, and it lay open on her computer desk.

He shifted his eyes to her. "Did you buy that book, or was it given to you?"

"Why? It's really an interesting book about..."

"I repeat. Bought or given?"

She flashed back to the image of him scolding Gloria as if she was his child. "Excuse me, I'm not 17 years old. Don't talk to me like that."

He seemed shocked. "Tempest, I just asked a simple question."

Then she did something she hadn't done in a very long time. She lied. "I bought it. And another one by the same man."

Michael's features hardened. "You bought them."

Yes." Tempest tilted her chin, daring him to argue the point.

Michael stepped close to her and very softly, stated," You are a poor liar," before walking out the front door, slamming it behind him.

Instinct told her to reach Paul and tell him what just happened. She had his card...but would Michael really do anything?

Paul closed his bible, thinking hard about the Song of Solomon. His understanding was clearer now. Women had much power over men,..much power. They seldom knew how much though. He chuckled at that thought. Tempest often had lunch with him, and discussed what she read of interest in Tabor's books. Each time he saw her, she seemed more beautiful? No, something more.

She insinuated herself into his life without even trying, even though she claimed to love Michael. Protecting her from danger was becoming secondary to having her for himself,..and he knew that was wrong.

He got up and headed for his bedroom, when he saw it.
The mans image stood in the doorway, long blonde hair blowing in an unseen wind. Paul froze, for a fleeting second thinking Michael was in his house. But the more he stared, he could see it was an image, not real.

Michael's face was filled with malice. Hatred sparkled in his eyes. His sneering mouth moved, silent. He raised his hand to point at Paul.

"Enough with the parlor tricks! You're capable of more, we both know that. Come and ring the bell, or get out of my house!" Closing his eyes, Paul pushed both arms out forcefully toward Michaels image. "Be gone! You are uninvited!" When he opened his eyes, the image was gone. The phone began to ring shrilly, breaking his reverie.

Answering it, he was pleased to hear Tempest on the other end. But he also knew this call was somehow connected to Michael's appearance. "Hey. To what do I owe this honor?"

Her laugh was music to his ears. "Let's just say I was worried about you. Maybe my fears are unfounded, but Michael saw one of the books you gave me. He got upset, and asked where I got them. I told him that I bought them."

"Don't ever lie to him about me again, okay?"

"I couldn't help it. He's so unreasonable where you're concerned."

"Don't you wonder why?"

"He knows you don't like him."

Paul laughed. "That's putting it mildly. Just don't lie about me anymore. Promise?"

She was silent, so he pressed the receiver tight to his ear. "Tempest...".

"Okay...okay! I promise."

Paul considered a little out of body visit of his own to Michael. Just to show him he wasn't the only one able to threaten from a distance, the coward.

"Paul...you still there?"

He cleared his mind. "I'm always here pumpkin. I told you that."

"Why Paul? Why are you there for me when you barely know me?"

"I know you well enough to care about you a great deal."Careful..change the subject.Don't push her. "How far have you gotten in the book?"

"Halfway. Either Tabor Ashe was a demon or an angel. His ideas are hard to swallow. Reality isn't reality. Dreams are alternative living. And the spoken word holds such power.He says if you state something without any doubt, with a firm mind, then you speak it into being. I think Michael practices that law. He's trying to work it on me now, but i'm trying to prove that another strong mind can resist. A stupid game really."

Paul felt elated. She was pulling away from his will. Wonderful."What are you resisting, Tempest?"

"He wants me to move in with him."

"Resist damn hard. Don't rush it."

Very softly, she whispered.." I'm real confused, Paul."

"About what?"

"About....you."

"Listen. Don't say any more...just..."

"I want to see you Paul. Can I come by?"

He felt a rush of emotions. To have her here, alone.

"Tempest...honestly...if you come here tonight, I can't promise to behave myself."

" Well honestly,..I have to find out if I can...behave myself."

Paul felt so vulnerable. More afraid than Michael ever made him.

"I'll try one more time. Remember I asked you not to let me read you? Well, i'm asking you to hang up right now."

She was quiet for awhile. Then she was there again, her voice firm with resolve. "Where do you live Paul?"

Tempest drove carefully, filled with unease. She had the strange sensation that someone was watching her. It was unnerving. Why are you doing this, she wondered, doesn't Michael satisfy you? He satisfied her, exhausted her, filled her mind with secrets,..but somehow he didn't touch her.

He was beautiful to look at, but he didn't look at her as if she was beautiful. He seemed to view her mind instead. Could that be why she melted when Paul looked at her? Because his eyes lingered on her face so lovingly? Maybe if she spent time with Paul alone, she'd know why she loved one man, but wanted another!

When Tempest parked before Paul's apartment building, the feeling of being watched increased. Getting out of her car and smoothing her long skirt, she looked up and down the street, half expecting Michael to appear. He must be wondering where she was, or knowing him, had an idea where she was. That chilled her, along with a pang of guilt. She considered getting back into her car and going home. I'm just visiting a good friend. Nothing will happen. Then why was there a knot in her stomach? Why was it so hard to climb the three steps and ring his bell? Taking a deep breath to calm herself, she climbed the steps, took one last look around, and rang his bell. The buzzer opened the door right away. She entered the hallway, which smelled of bleach and lemon, and noticed two large buckets and mops along the wall. It was so clean.

As she climbed the stairs toward the third floor, she heard him call down,"That you Tempest?"

"Coming!" She reached his open door and stepped in to find him standing there holding a large bowl of popcorn. He grinned like a kid. "You nut!" Tempest laughed, and took a handful of popcorn. He looked at her from top to bottom as if unsure she was really there. Warmth filled her.

"You're beautiful," he said simply, before leading her into the living room.

His place had a comfortable feel, just like he did. Paul wore jeans, a tee shirt, and was barefoot. She'd never really noticed his build before. But it was obvious that he worked out. Not as slender as Michael, more bulked. Stop it, she chastised herself, blushing.

He plopped on his soft leather couch and pat the spot next to him. She noted that his decor was all black,lamps, chairs, and it surprised her. Sitting next to him, she noticed a large picture hanging above his t.v. It was of an Archangel, glowing and virile, holding a huge sword which flashed lightening. Beautiful.

"That's an odd picture for you to have."

"Why, it's an Archangel? A warrior Angel. I call him my relative...hahaha."

She looked at him, ready to tease about that statement, but he was looking at her so intensely that the words died in her throat.

"You always wear dresses or skirts. That's kind of sweet, in an old fashioned way."

Blushing, she looked at the picture again. It seemed to be watching them. This was ridiculous. "Paul...tell me about yourself. You are this big mystery. How long have you been in Boston? How old are you? Tell me about your religion."

"Whoa...all of that?"

"Yeah..try."

"Alright then."

Tempest felt herself sinking into the comfortable couch, growing more conscious of his nearness with each passing minute. Kicking off her shoes, she tucked her feet up under her, anxious to know more about him.

Leaning back, Paul began. "I was adopted. They say I was abandoned at the hospital, and I was adopted very quickly, by a nurse and her husband. They were great and I know they loved me...but ...well I was too much for them. I was seeing strange things all the time. An imaginary friend, this little girl, came to keep me company every night. I think I scared them."

For a while, Paul looked at her strangely. "Damn...I just realized, she looked like you."

Tempest bit her lower lip, unnerved by that revelation.

"Anyway," he continued, " when I turned ten, they sent me here from Virginia, to stay with my gram. This sweet, loving old lady with so much patience. She accepted me for what I was, and helped me deal with it all, as much as she could.

She died four years ago and that's when I began working at the shop. My gram and Maggie were friends from church."

He pressed a kernel of popcorn into her mouth and watched her chew. "I just turned thirty, so i've been in Boston for twenty years."

Tempest smiled at him, totally relaxed. Listening to him talk was comforting. His voice reminded her of a flowing river somehow, deep...quiet.

He took her hand in his, rubbed his thumb around her palm. "I have one idea about my religion. I think all of earth's religion has a bit of the truth in them. All religions are right...but they are also wrong. My inner voice is my religion. I trust the God within me,..nothing else." Closing his hand around hers, Paul teased, "Your turn."

Tempest felt as if all of her nerves were centered in her hand..where he held it so easily. It was getting hard to breathe.

"Okay,..I was born during a huge storm twenty eight years ago. Lightening struck the hospital. My Scottish mother said I was a Tempest, and named me that. I wasn't schooled in any religion. My father taught me to respect the earth, and others. My parents died a year and a half ago. I still can't believe they're gone."

"I know..."

She couldn't contain it anymore. "Paul,..I think of you a lot. And Michael knows it."

"Just like he knows that I love you?"

Stunned, Tempest looked at him for any sign of teasing. There was none.

He continued,"I need to tell you something. Just before you called me, I had a visitor of sorts. I saw an image of Michael right here in this apartment. He was very pissed. It was some kind of threat, I guess."

"That,..that's not possible."

"Yes it is, Pumpkin, for him. So whatever transpires between us..he'll probably know."

"You're scaring me, Paul."

"I just want you to be aware."

She whispered, "You don't want to see me anymore?"

Paul sighed, "I don't know what the hell i'm saying," before pulling her close, and covering her mouth with his. The kiss was passionate, hungry, and tender,..all at the same time. Tempest drowned in it, like sinking into honey. His arms around her felt so right. She felt safe. He lay back, pulling her atop him as they sank into the soft cushions.

Yes, it was different. Her head was clear. She felt each touch of his hands,..heated brands on her flesh. He touched all of her, setting her on fire. Amazed, Tempest looked down into his passion stricken face. He was so handsome. Full, chiseled features, dark eyes, which looked up at her hungrily.

They stared at each other for tense moments, as if unable to believe it could be this way for them. Then thought ended, giving way to instinct. Each removed the clothing of the other. Tempest gave herself to him with free will, kissing, tasting, exploring, discovering all of him as he did the same to her. Together, they rocked, their lovemaking like a symphony, slowly building to a crescendo which shattered them both, leaving them trembling in its wake.

Tempest cried. Into his bare chest, she cried, unable to stop. Not really understanding why the tears fell.

Paul held her tight, rubbing her back in soothing circles, kissing her neck, tasting her tears. He knew why she cried because he hadn't expected it either.

Perfection.

CHAPTER THIRTEEN

Michael held Tempests obsidian ball, standing in his kitchen, alone. He could feel them,..as a sense of losing control. As if she was slipping away,and very happy! He threw the globe across the kitchen where it shattered a glass cabinet and several peices of china. Picking up a butcher knife on the table, he stabbed it into the wall, almost to its hilt. He scattered the food he'd prepared across the table with a swipe of his arm. Chicken, rice, brocolli. Did she really think she could deceive him? He knew where she was as surely as he felt the abrupt loosening of his control. What had gone wrong?

Enraged, he kicked a chair over. The clatter echoed in the empty house. That bastard Paul, his adversary, that is what had gone wrong! Obviously, he needed a stronger incentive to leave Tempest alone.

Michael stalked through the kitchen, entered the shop and stood at its large windows, trying to think. To be rational. He wasn't fool enough to think she loved him. He made her feel she did, but it was a suggestion, an order. He was puzzled. Wasn't it a strong suggestion? She always ended up beneath him, wrapped in his arms. What was it about Paul that reached her heart, beyond his control? Could he really be that strong,a hidden strength that he only chose to use now? Paul had warned him not to understimate him.

A cold decision presented itself. No Paul, no more problem. Tempest would succumb easily again, behave, and get down to business. Important time was being wasted!

Tempest stood in the shower with Paul, her eyes red from crying. He soaped her back, massaged her shoulders.

"You feel better, honey?"

she nodded, now able to think. Turning to face him, she smiled and he visibly relaxed.

Hugging her, Paul kissed the tip of her nose. "It'll be alright. Don't cry about us." He left the shower first, handed her a towel, and left the bathroom.

She wanted to tell him she didn't cry about what had happened between them. Or about how he made her feel. She had never felt so peaceful...so happy. He had tenderly touched her somewhere inside that she never knew existed. When she made love to him, she was totally naked...inside. And she wasn't afraid of her nakedness. No, she cried because she didn't know what to do. How could she be like this with Paul, but feel she had to be with Michael? What kind of woman behaves this way? She fought fresh tears, ashamed of herself. Why couldn't she make a choice? It didn't make sense! She dried herself and wrapped the towel around her, then went to find Paul. He was sprawled on the couch, wearing a pair of sweatpants...waiting for her by the look he gave .

He sat up. "C'mere, pumpkin. Don't look so afraid."

"I'm not afraid of you. I'm afraid of myself."

He gave her a look of such warmth and compassion, that she practically ran to him. He settled her in his lap, stroked her damp hair. "Listen to me. You, Michael, I...what we are going through now, it is a blood thing, and can't be prevented. It can't be stopped just like that. It must run its course. This is a test for you, Tempest. One you must go through. It will be hard. Because your blood remembers things that you do not. It requires things from you that can't be ignored. You have to be strong, sweetie."

"I don't understand. And how can I feel the need to be with both you and Michael. That makes me a horrible person!"

He laughed dryly, almost painfully. "You won't want both of us always. You'll make a choice, because you have to. I won't use Michael's methods, draw you to me with the force of my will. I will trust, and let your will bring you to me."

Snuggling against his warm body, Tempest shuddered and closed her eyes. The blood remembers...what did that mean?

If she was at Michael's, she'd be sitting at a table with him, learning to focus and use her mind. He'd have her at the window, telling her to read people that walked by, unknowing. Or reading one of his books on meditation, scrying, control. Maybe they'd be in bed making violent love.

They would never snuggle like she was now, with Paul. No quiet, restful moments for them. With Paul, she could imagine lazy days, just being together. Having him grow into an important part of her, and she of him. Contentment. Shouldn't that be enough? He had things to teach her too...gently as he did most things.

When Paul picked her up and carried her to his bedroom, strangely like Michael's because of the black decor, she didn't resist. Instead, she curled against him, feeling at peace for the first time since the death of her parents.

Paul opened his eyes to see Michael standing over the bed. His hand was bent into a claw, and that claw was descending to his chest. Death! He mustn't touch his heart!

Reaching up, Paul grabbed his wrist in a tight grip, fighting to stop its descent. A cold smile touched Michael's face and though his lips moved, no sound came out. Incantations. His hand was mere inches from Pauls chest, where his heart beat frantically. Michael had the advantage of standing, pressing down.

"Yahweh! Help me!," Paul cried out, using both hands to grab hold of

Michaels wrist. The muscles in his arms trembled with the exertion. Slowly, he gained an advantage. "It won't be this easy," Paul promised, and then there was the loud snap of breaking bone.

Michael looked surprised and then his mouth formed a silent scream. Just as suddenly as he appeared, he was gone.

"Paul! Paul...wake up! Please, honey!" He woke up to Tempest shaking him. She looked terrified. He could feel the sweat on his face and chest. A quick look around revealed they were alone.

Tempest watched him closely, feeling all kinds of emotions rolling off him in waves. Must have been some nightmare! "Paul, are you okay? You were talking in your sleep and struggling. What were you dreaming about?"

Disoriented, he looked at her. His arms and wrists throbbed painfully. "Just a nightmare." he whispered. "And don't you have to go to work?" Daylight was filtering in through the drapes.

Reality flooded back to her. "Oh, I really do have to go." Kissing him, she considered taking a sick day.

Paul rubbed noses with her and teased," I know you have to go. I'll make coffee." He got up and went to the kitchen while she dressed. The pain in his arms subsided a bit, but he needed to be more alert. Make his home secure. Michael was getting in too easily, and now he could expect anything. Things had taken a serious turn, as it was clear Michael wanted him dead.

Tempest came in the kitchen and found Paul preparing a mug of wonderfully fragrant coffee for her. There wasn't much time for her to get home, shower, dress, and get to work, so the invigorating drink was very welcome. She placed a piece of paper with her work phone number on the counter

before taking the mug of coffee. "I hate to go."

"I understand, sweetie. Now get going or you'll be late." He walked her to the door, then kissed her deeply. "Tempest. Don't go crazy trying to rationalize things. We'll talk."

She kissed him again before running down the stairs. From below she called up to him..."I'll keep reading. Promise." Then the door slammed, and Paul felt her absence deep inside.

Closing his door, Paul returned to his bedroom. Going into the closet, he located a leather satchel and carried it to the bed. Opening it, he removed a small glass bottle of blessed water, a very aged bible, and a pouch of dried desert sage.

Reverently , he opened the bible to Psalms 59, Davids prayer of protection. First he walked to the front door and poured a thin stream of holy water across the threshold. While doing so he read the Psalm. He then crumbled some dried sage there as well. He repeated this ritual at all entranceways to his apartment, including the windows.

When this was done, he returned everything to the satchel and put it back in the closet. Paul went to his dresser, and in a bottom drawer, reached behind the socks to press the wood, and it popped open to reveal a hidden compartment. He pulled out a small wooden box. Opening it, he took out a roll of parchment, very old but well cared for. Carefully, he unrolled it to reveal a smaller version of the Archangel picture in his living room. The image was surrounded by symbols and lines that resembled hebrew. He rubbed his hands across the script lovingly. "Uriel," he said softly. "Our blood is one. Hear me, one of your own. Help me through this, relation, fallen no more. Forgiveness is at hand. Selah!

The room filled with a beautiful purple haze, filled with flecks of golden light. Paul fell to his knees, stretched out his arms, and was silent.

CHAPTER FOURTEEN

Tempest sat at her desk, adding figures, losing herself in the numbers. She didn't want to think right now. At noon time she received a visitor. Michael. In a way, she'd known he would show up. Right away, she noticed the brace on his right wrist. "What happened?"

Giving her a smile that didn't quite reach his eyes, he replied, " An accident. Grease on the kitchen floor. I slipped."

"Is it broken?"

"Hairline fracture. Will you stop by tonight?"

Consumed by guilt, Tempest avoided his eyes. "I'm not sure, Michael." She moved some papers, put pencils in the pencil cup, all the time aware that he simply stood there, watching her.

"Tempest. Look at me."

She met his eyes, and immediatly felt ill. Her stomach churned and her head began to ache. His ice blue eyes glued to hers, she felt as if she wanted to sleep. Weak. "Of course i'll be over. I'll be over right after work."

Placing his good hand on her desk, he leaned toward her."How is it possible that the honest woman I was attracted to has changed so,..drastically?"

Tearing her eyes away from his frosty blue ones, she trembled inwardly.

"Little one, remember this. What is done in the dark always comes to light."

Near tears, she whispered,"So...you know."

"Know what?"

"Don't play games with me Michael." She waited, unable to look at those eyes, his face cold again.

" Did you ever think that Paul could be the evil one in all this? That he might have plans for you? After all, I just offer to help you learn. Why would he compromise you, knowing we are together? Think about that, and I'll see you tonight."

Tempest watched him leave, her heart beating erratically. He hid it well, but Michael was furious. Why wouldn't he be?

But she had gone to Paul, had called him. He'd even tried to warn her away. No...he wasn't evil, no way. Thinking was painful. She'd cheated on one man, had another man hanging. What in the hell was wrong with her? How could she behave like this? It was like her life was on automatic, and she had lost all control!

The moon was full. Tempest sat in her car and stared at it. Lilac clouds seemed to cover its brilliance, but it's light still enhanced the street. She was hesitant to enter Odds and Ends.

Guilt was eating at her. Michael knew, just as Paul had warned her. She didn't regret going to Paul, but she felt so guilty. Gathering her courage, she got out and finding the door unlocked, went inside.

Candles burned everywhere. On the windowsills, the tables. There was a large circle of stones on the shop floor.
Circumventing them, Tempest went in the kitchen. Bottles and piles of herbs or flowers sat on the table, and something boiled on the stove. The aroma wasn't exactly...pleasant. She noticed one of the glass cabinet doors was broken. Something inside urged her to leave, now. But curiousity won out. Well this is dramatic. Someones been watching too many movies.

Michael came down from his room and entered the kitchen. Seeing her, he nodded. "You came." He wore a black sweatsuit, and heavy necklace of precious stones. His golden hair was loose, and once more, she was struck by how handsome he was. Too bad he was so aloof with her now, but what had she expected?

Michael quickly walked to her, grabbed a handful of hair and painfully jerked her head back, exposing her neck. Placing his mouth at the base of her neck, he gently nipped her.

She froze, stunned by this unexpected attack.

"If you weren't so important to me, I'd rip your throat out," he whispered, before kissing the same spot. Releasing her hair, he stepped away.

Rubbing her neck, Tempest tried to calm herself. That threat had been much too real.

He smiled coldly. "Don't you love me, Tempest?" Before she could answer, he continued, "You're reading the books of Tabor Ashe,..my old teacher. I'm sure you were aware of that. I will show you his teachings in action."

Although a little afraid, she followed him into the shop.
Michael sat cross legged in the stone circle. "Join me," he ordered.
Tempest did as told, and sat opposite him.

"The circle represents completion. Outside of the circle is the unknown. All the things the spiritual man seeks. Within the circle is knowledge. All the things the spiritual man is given. I sit in the center and offer you knowledge. I am not the One who knows all things, but my knowledge is great. My teacher once told me to seek, always seek. But recognize that which you find. I have found knowledge, and recognize it in others."

Tempest had the fleeting thought that Michael was just a glory seeker, filled with self gratification. Just as quickly, she mused, who am I to judge? What do I know?

"Tempest," he looked angry, "It's time to travel."

Tabor Ashe had written in depth about Astral travel, so she knew this is what he meant. "I've never done it before."

"I know, but tonight you will. Not the baby steps of fledglings, to the sky and back. Oh no, we will visit a focus."

A tingle of excitement filled her. "What will we see?"

Michael stared at her for a tense moment, the hint of a smirk on his face. "Not where, but who." His smile broadened, and she felt a chill to the soul. "We are going to visit Maggies shop,..and Paul."

Her excitement was replaced with dread. Michael wanted to spy on Paul. She didn't want to do that! "No,..I can't do that."

"Why not? He'll never know. He won't even sense our presence."

"We can go somewhere e....."

"No. We'll visit Paul. Now focus with me."

CHAPTER FIFTEEN

Tempest knew it was wrong, felt it to the depth of her being. But the prospect of being able to astral travel thrilled her. She looked directly into Michael's eyes, his pupils. He stared at her just as deeply.

She watched the dark pupils of his eyes expand, surrounded by vivid blue. How strange.

"Breathe," he instructed. "Three deep, cleansing breaths. Deep in, slowly out. And focus on my eyes. Don't be afraid. Visualize Maggies Shop. Remember the smells, the way it feels to be there. The sounds. Let those images fill your mind. Focus, breathe,..relax."

Michael sounded strange to her, slow and disjointed. Tempest still did as he instructed. She soon felt a drowsiness overtake her. It was so quiet. When she thought of Maggies, Paul automatically came to mind. His pleasant scent, endearing smile. Those dark, kind eyes. Then Michael's eyes seemed to change, to become dark and kind like Pauls. She felt as if she was falling, and then she was gazing down at the circle, at her and Michael.

We look dead, she thought, looking down, watching them grow

smaller and smaller still within the circle. I'm floating!

Tempest was filled with joy. She sensed someone close by, heard them whisper, "Don't panic."

In a second, they were in Paul's office. The quickness of it amazed her. Paul was with a client, discussing her reading. Again she heard Michael's voice, although she couldn't see him. "Go near. He won't know. Touch him."

Surprised that she could control her movements, Tempest walked to Paul and placed her hand on his shoulder. Feelings flooded her, so many feelings, the strongest being love. Warm, encompassing love for everyone, and all things. Total, unconditional love. Her hand tingled and she saw it was inside of his shoulder, not on it.

Paul stood up, suddenly alert. He slowly glanced around the room. "Tempest...?" It was a whispered question. He seemed to look right at her!

Tempest felt a strong tug in the chest area, and then she was no longer in Paul's office, but at Michael's, rapidly descending to her still body within the circle.

Joining with her body was so rapid and sudden, that Tempest felt shocked and disoriented. Her heavy limbs could hardly move, and the loss of that incredible freedom made her want to cry. I really did it!

Michael watched her, expressionless. A sheen of sweat covered his

face. His eyes lingered on her face, fell to her chest, then to her face
again.   "We did it," she
whispered, excited. Her heart raced. And Paul had known they were
there! Michael had been wrong, because Paul knew she was there!

Still silent, Michael stood and left the circle to begin dousing the
candles. He didn't seem to share her excitement, but then again, Tempest
reasoned, it wasn't his first out of body experience. Anxious to break the
heavy silence, she asked, "Do you want me to gather these stones
together?"

"Sure. There's a pouch on the counter."

She retrieved the pouch and carefully placed the stones inside. When
that was done, she looked for Michael, but he wasn't in the room. After a
search of the kitchen and upstairs, Tempest realized he wasn't in the
house at all.

"Michael!" No reply. Running to the front windows, she looked out to
see both their cars parked. Where was he?

Paul purified his cards with smoke from a braid of sweetgrass, put
them in their pouch, and locked them in his desk.

What had happened earlier tonight? He had felt a presence. Tempests
presence to be exact, and it had been strong. It seemed her lessons were
progressing. Reaching into his left pants pocket, he caressed the crystal
and onyx stones there reassuringly. Protection. Paul locked his office and

waved at Maggie as he passed her in the lobby. Thank goodness he was parked right around the corner. He felt tired. Walking to his car, his mind wandered to Tempest again. He needed to call her.

When his car was in view he saw he had company. Michael leaned against his car, holding something in his hand. He waved with a braced hand, and Paul remembered his attack at the house. So,...he had injured him.

As Paul walked toward him, he could see what Michael was holding. It was a long cylinder of crystal. The stem was decorated with beads of opal and quartz. At the top was a ruby globe set on a piece of obsidian. A wand. The man held a wand! His first impulse was to laugh at the gaudy tool, but he stifled it, knowing better than to underestimate the man. In the right hands a wand could be a powerful channel for energy.

Reaching the car, Paul walked around him to open the door. "What do you want?"

Michael pointed the wand at him, closed his eyes, and began to speak. Startled, Paul reached out to shove the wand away, but Michael's grip was steady. "I have come to say your days are numbered and few. I have lost all patience with you."

Speechless, Paul watched Michael lose substance, grow thin as rice paper dancing on an unseen breeze, before vanishing altogether. His hair rose on his neck and arms. Closing the car door, he decided it wasn't a good idea to drive, and hailed a cab. Getting in, he gave his address and settled for the ride home. His safety zone. As an afterthought, he fastened the seatbelt. Concentrate on the Most High, he cautioned himself. Don't give the curse substance. He looked out the window at the dark homes lit within, festive at night when the grime was invisible.

When they exited onto the MassPike, the driver began to talk loudly. Paul listened to him, an inner alarm ringing a warning. "I hate this damn city. I do man! A damn ride to nowhere, that's what it is!"

Trying to let the man know he was just having a bad day, Paul replied, "Nothing's all bad. Even taxachusetts."

"What the hell you know? My wife left me this week. My kids don't even want to see me! Can't make ends meet, shit!"
The drivers voice rose excitedly and he almost swerved into the wrong lane before righting himself.

Paul realized he'd made a mistake. A mud colored cloud seemed to surround the drivers body. He looked into the rear view mirror to see the man watching him with red, glazed eyes. Forcing himself to sound calm, Paul suggested, "You can let me out here."

"Oh no, bastard. All of you bastards try to stiff me and run without payin'! Trying to rob me...the working man! I've lost patience with all of you! I've lost patience!"

Paul felt ill as Michaels words rang from the drivers mouth. The man hit the gas, accelerating, and the force flung Paul back against the seat. A small sombrero hanging from the rear view mirror danced in a crazy pivot. At high speed, they crossed into oncoming traffic. Realizing what was about to happen, Paul braced himself.

A red SUV slammed into them, spinning the cab across the median. Another car hit them in the side with such force that together the car and taxi skidded across the highway to rest on an incline of brush and dirt. The sounds of crunching metal and breaking glass filled Paul's ears as pain wracked his violently tossed body. Weak, he whispered, "Thy will be done," before blackness consumed him.

CHAPTER SIXTEEN

Tempest looked up from the sandwich she was eating at the kitchen table. There hadn't been a sound, but Michael stood in the doorway, looking pale and tired.

"Where were you?"

"I was here."

"No you weren't! I looked everywhere."

With a raised brow, he asked, "Did you look in the basement? I store many of my things down there."

She calmed a bit, but not entirely. "The basement? Well couldn't you hear me calling you?"

"Not really." Michael sat, his entire body tense.

She tried to read him but it was useless. "What kind of reply is that? Didn't you know i'd worry about where you were?"

He shrugged "Your actions show you don't care too much for me lately. Have you touched me? Kissed me? Have we made love?"

Guiltily she looked away from him. " I still care about you.. it's just that i'm confused."

Pain.

Tempest was filled with it so suddenly that she couldn't breathe. It's intensity crippled her. She fell from the chair, curled into a tight ball, and cried out in agony. Taking shallow breaths, she looked up at Michael with pain glazed eyes.

Alarm was written all over his face. He scooped her up in his arms and carried her up to his bed. "What is it sweetheart, what's wrong?!" He lay her down as gently as possible, but another spasm gripped her, violently attacking all of her nerves. She screamed in agony, her face wet with tears.

Michael leaned close. "Tell me what is happening?"

She could barely talk because of the agony filling her being. "Pain...help me." It was a mere gasp, but he heard her, and fled the room. As she lay, rocking and moaning, the pain began to ease. It was replaced by a soreness in her limbs, but the pain was definitely going. Breathing easier, she dared to stretch out.

Michael returned with a cup of hot liquid and carefully helped her drink it. There wasn't much taste, but it was thick, and she wanted to gag. "Do you feel better?"

"Yes. Good Lord. What happened to me!?"

Stroking her damp hair from her face, he grew thoughtful. "Where was the pain?"

"Everywhere." She shuddered. "My stomach, legs, and especially my chest. I thought I was dying." Stunned, she saw a hint of a grin on his face. "Did you do this to me?"

"Don't be silly. Must be an affect you suffered from astraling. Your shocked system must be repairing itself."

"I never heard of anyone suffering like that from out of body."

"But sweetie..you are not average."

He's lying. The knowledge was so firm in her mind that when he reached for her, she moved away. "What's really wrong with me?"

"Exactly what I told you." Setting the cup on the floor , he sat on the bed beside her, the image of concern. "Why do you think I'll hurt you?"

She took a deep breath. "Because you know i've...i've been with Paul. I don't think you're the forgive and forget type."

Michael seemed amused. "How intuitive of you. I'm not. But i'm willing to make allowances where you're concerned. I care very much for you."

Tempest stared at him. Had she ever met anyone else so cocky and sure of themselves? It was time to lay all the cards on the table. "Do you know what's strange Michael? When I first met you, in my office, I got very sick. I know it doesn't make sense." She watched him for a reaction, but there was none. "I mean, you were so handsome and I was powerfully attracted to you, but...then I got this foul scent and felt so sick. Why would that happen?"

"Why do you think that would happen?"

Thier eyes locked. "You felt evil Michael. Darkness was in you. "

"Am I evil Tempest?" He leaned closer to her. "Are you sick now?"

" No, " she admitted.

" Does that make sense?"

"No...it doesn't."

Michael grazed her cheek with a kiss."Do I still attract you?"

Her stomach knotted, she stood up. "When I look into those cursed eyes of yours..I'm not myself at all. I'm going home Michael. I have to think and...well, it's been quite a night."

" Has it now?" He lay across the bed, a broad smile on his face. "Then go, see yourself out. Think. You are mines Tempest, i'm never letting you go." He rolled over and grinned up at her. "If you see our friend Paul, tell him hello for me."

Chilled by those words, she raced out of the room and down the stairs, not feeling safe until she was in her car. She headed home, wanting...needing to put distance between them.

*   *   *

The tunnel. It stretched before him, the walls moving liquidly, like heavy smoke or murky water. He travelled the tunnel, aware of someone at his side walking with him. Far in the distance glowed a familiar light, so bright and warm and welcoming. The person with him spoke, and he instantly recognized the voice as one he'd heard all his life. One that guided him.

"Paul. You cannot go."

" I want to. I'm so tired. It's been so long."

" We understand, but you cannot go. You are not done yet."

Paul looked toward that light and it felt like home. He wanted to go home!

"I feel i've forgotten my purpose. What isn't done?"

He suddenly felt enveloped in the most love filled hug he could imagine, and his eyes filled with tears.

"Two have not become one. And the one is loved."

Then he was alone. The light began to fade, and the pain.
Like electricity, pain travelled his body, touching every organ and limb. With a loud moan, Paul opened his eyes. He was laying on a cold table in a very bright room. It hurt his eyes.
Strangers in white stood all around him. Concerned faces wearing masks. "We got him!" one man shouted, his white gown stained with

blood.

Fighting some kind of restraints on his arms, Paul flailed, the pain more than he could bear.

There was an order to sedate him, and a clear mask was shoved gently over his face. Paul choked once before darkness descended...and peace.

Tempest sat on her couch with Tabor Ashe's second book on her lap. Tucking her feet up under her, she thought about the painful bout at Michaels house. There was something to it, she just knew it! At first she was convinced he had done it to her...but now she wasn't so sure. Grabbing the cordless phone from beside her, she dialed Paul's number. It rang and rang. Ten times, no answer. Peeking up at the clock, she saw it was a bit after three a.m. Where could he be? Worry reared its head, but she fought it. There was alot about his life she didn't know. He could be anywhere, doing anything.

The first book had been full of uses for herbs, minerals, and objects. Or mind strengthening stories and excercises. Some biblical references, and arguments against wideheld belief systems. She opened this volume, and the first page had a paragraph titled, The Watchers. Grigori among us. Frowning, she thought the phrase familiar. The names tugged at her memory, but she couldn't place it. Hmmn.

Reading further, she frowned.

The Grigori, also known as the watchers are angels which were given the task to aid man when God created thier species. They became enamored of the new species, mankind and made the choice with free will to become as them. They taught man the forbidden arts of magic with herbs, reading the stars, divination, and sorcery. The watchers married human women and had children with them. All these things were against the orders of God.

It is said that the great flood was created to wipe out these angelic/human offspring. ..

Tempest sat forward, her heart racing. What had Paul told her..the blood? No..no they were wiped out. She tried to calm herself. Of course she was over reacting . It was insane. She continued to read.

These Watchers, Grigori, Fallen ones, appealed to Enoch to mediate in thier behalf with God. But they were bound for seventy generations for thier disobedience. What I have come to know, and mean to reveal to any who would listen, is that all these offspring were not destroyed. Thier blood lines continue. The Vatican protects these files jealously. Those of the blood line are known, and numbered. This must speak to you, because you are studying, searching. I, Tabor Ashe, want to answer your questions.

Tempest collapsed back against the couch, her heart racing. Had Paul given her these books for a reason more than understanding Michael?

She needed to talk to him!

Again she called him...but no answer. Paul, honey, where are you!? Closing the book, she shut her eyes. Tabor Ashe was a madman. Who could believe all of this? Her life was so crazy right now, well...she was ripe to believe anything. I need to calm down, be reasonable. Paul, get home.

Tempest called again at five, and there still wasn't an answer. That is when she became truly worried. As if in dreams, she remembered being unable to find Michael, the pain she endured. She remembered his parting words, "If you see our friend Paul, tell him hello for me."

Oh No! Michael, what have you done?!

CHAPTER SEVENTEEN

Tempest sat on the couch cradling the book in her lap, worrying about Paul until she finally fell into a fitful sleep. There were dreams. Dreams of fire, and vast blue sky, of lush gardens filled with trees bearing fruit, of laughter.

She woke to the alarm blaring from her bedroom. Soaked with sweat, and suffering from a mild headache, she called Paul right away. It rang hollowly, unanswered. She made a decision. She'd stop by Maggie's, and hopefully, Paul would be there, or they'd know where he was. If not, then she would go see Michael, and somehow force him to tell her what he'd done. The latter prospect terrified her and seemed doomed to failure, but if she had to...

After a quick shower, and dressing, she drove past Paul's apartment building, hoping to find his car parked outside. When it wasn't, she continued in to town to Maggie's.

Tempest was beginning to panic. Like a wild animal, struggling in her chest to break free, panic was getting stronger. What if Paul was dead? How could she live, knowing it was her fault?! She'd brought nothing but trouble to him. How could she go on without ever feeling his touch again? Tears flooding her eyes, she could barely see the road.

As she neared the shop she passed Paul's car, parked around the corner. Thank goodness! He was at Maggie's after all! It took a while to find a parking space, and when she did she practically ran to the shop, and burst through the doors leading to the lobby.

Maggie was standing at her desk in the midst of her regular psychics, as well as some clients. Some of them were sobbing, some talking excitedly.

Tempest froze. No, it can't be. Not Paul...

Mona noticed her first, and the anger on her face was feral. "Tempest? Why are you here? What the hell do you want?"

Tempest wanted to grab the small woman and wring her neck. This was no time for jealousy! The bitch!

Maggie gently pushed Mona aside, and came over to Tempest. "Do you know?"

"Something's happened to Paul?"

It was clear that Maggie had been crying. She touched Tempest on the shoulder. " I got a call early this morning. Paul is in critical condition at Mass General Hospital. For some reason, he took a cab last night, and they got into a very bad accident on the highway. The driver died, and Paul was badly hurt. He lost a lot of blood because of an injury to his chest, pierced by some metal, but they stopped the bleeding. The other injuries weren't as serious. I went up and saw him and he's resting."

Unable to hold it in any longer, Tempest began to cry. The silent tears slid down her face, and she could only stare at Maggie, unable to believe it . Paul...her Paul...hurt.

Maggie looked at her, disbelief written all over her face.
"You do care for him? I thought so. " She hugged Tempest, and whispered so the others couldn't hear. "You watch out for that Michael person, you hear me? Paul is on the 6th floor intensive care. Tell them you're his sister."

When she stepped away, Tempest nodded and left.

Something cold was wiped on Paul's wrist, waking him. It was followed by the pinch of a new intravenous needle. Paul's eyes felt too heavy to open, but his other senses were alert. He could hear the drip of an IV, the whispers of his doctor and nurse.

Sticky electrodes on his chest made him itch, as well as the tight wrapping around his ribs, and leg. His catheter hurt despite the sedative, and his head hurt most of all.

"Paul...Paul Carson...can you hear me?"

He wanted to ignore them and retreat again into sleep. Instead, he forced his eyes open and stared up at the kind eyes of his doctor. They were full of concern. "Can you understand me Paul?"

Paul nodded slightly, not wanting to make his headache worse.

"Good, very good." The doctor smiled and motioned to the nurse. "We removed the respirator early this morning because you are breathing very well on your own. Do you remember anything about the accident?"

The accident. He remembered all of it. The driver ...being hit and spinning out..the crunch of metal. Again, he nodded.

"It was a very bad accident, Paul. Metal from the wreck punctured your chest, just missing your heart and nicking a major artery. You lost a lot of blood. We thought we lost you. But it's repaired now, and all you need to do is rest and heal. You have two broken ribs, a bruised spleen, and a concussion. It could have been much worse. You're a lucky man."

Paul tried to speak, but the words seemed stuck in his throat, which felt dry and raw. His mind raced as he remembered who had caused the accident. Michael. What if he's hurt Tempest. What if he's lost patience with her as well?

The doctor shined a tiny light in his eyes, checked his chest dressing, and motioned to the nurse again. "Now rest. Don't try to talk. We called Maggie Justin, her number was in your wallet. She came up to see you, and said she will handle everything."

The nurse appeared at his side, and injected something into Paul's IV. He wanted to protest his medication, but sleep was claiming him already. He gave in to it's comfort.

Parking in a no parking zone, Tempest ran up the long circular driveway and into the hospital lobby. It was huge, full of sick patients, and visitors. Food trays were being shuffled back and forth to the many elevators. She took an elevator to the sixth floor and located the intensive care ward.

A nurse stopped her. "May I help you?"

"Yes, I just found out my brother ,Paul, was in a terrible accident and was brought here last night. Can I see him?"

The nurse nodded. "Wait here a moment please."

It was so quiet except for the sounds of monitors. Tempest waited, afraid of what she might see. Another nurse came and led her to a curtain. She opened the curtain and told her to go into the tiny area.

"We've been keeping him sedated," she said. "The chest injury is pretty serious, but we stopped the bleeding and it looks good. We lost him once, but he's a fighter, and we got him back. So don't be alarmed if he seems out of it."

Tempest could only nod, her chest tight. Once the nurse left, she approached the bed. She knew why she'd had the pain now. She had felt Paul's pain. When she reached him, she could barely breathe. This couldn't be Paul!

His face was so swollen and bruised she could barely recognize him. Tubes and wires snaked from many beeping, blinking monitors, trailed to him and disappeared under the sheet. A thin, transparent tube crossed his face, two prongs under his nostrils, to deliver oxygen.

Gently holding his hand, she just watched him, devastated. Michael...if you did this...i'll never forgive you. I'll hate you. Leaning close, she kissed Paul lightly on the lips, not wanting to hurt him. "I'm here sweetie. I'm right here."

Michael parked behind Paul's car. He sat behind the wheel, thinking things over. He was pretty sure that the pain Tempest had suffered was sympathy pain for Paul, which was good. But how badly was he hurt?

Getting out of his car, he walked the short distance to Maggie's shop, and went in. There was an air of sadness in the place, and he felt encouraged. Maggie sat at her desk, watching him with outright alarm. Wonderful.

Walking up to her, he greeted, "Hello Maggie. Is Paul around?"

She leaned back in her chair as if attempting to put more space between them. "No...he isn't."

"Maggie...maggie. Are you going to tell me what I need to know? Or do I have to drag it from your wrinkled throat?"

She cringed from the malice in his voice. "I have nothing to tell you."

Michael softened his voice. "I'm not in the mood for games." She trembled, satisfying him greatly. "Now, you stupid woman, tell me what I need to know." He looked into her eyes, smiling...waiting.

Maggie tried to look away, but she couldn't. "Wha..what do you want from me!"

"Use that little brain of yours. You know exactly what I want."

"I,..please, just leave."

Circling her desk, Michael bent, looking directly into her face. His smile was gone. "Listen, bitch. Tell me what I need to know, or you'll wish you were dead. Understand?"

Tears squeezed from her eyes, but she couldn't help herself. Maggie blurted,"Paul is alive at Mass General Hospital. Tempest is probably there."

Placing one finger between her eyes, he poked her hard. "Now, was that so hard?"

As Maggie sobbed softly, he walked outside. Paul was hospitalized. Good. Tempest was there. Intolerable!

There was the sensation of soreness, not quite pain. Opening his eyes, Paul tried to focus. A chair was pulled up to the side of his bed, and a woman slept there, slumped uncomfortably. Tempest. He managed a smile, relaxing within. She was here. Safe. Painfully, he spoke her name.

She woke instantly, reaching for his hand. "Shh..it's me. I'm here Paul. You must rest."

"It,..was Michael."

Anger filled her. Intense anger. "I suspected as much, sweetie. I'll be right here. You just get better."

He needed to tell her so much, but it was painful to speak. A small voice invaded his mind. "Heal yourself! Time is short!" Paul was startled. His inner voice had never been so commanding.

Tempest watched him. She was relieved to see some of the swelling had gone down. The bruises not quite as bright. She kissed his hand. "Paul, i'm so sorry. This is all my fault. My ego and vanity caused all of this. My need to know everything. But almost losing you...I know it's you I love."

Paul whispered. "Not your fault. Had no real choice. No guilt."

He smiled weakly at her. His eyes told her so much, and the tears came. She felt so much guilt, and nothing he could say would remove it. At the first party...she should have listened to him, and left.

He squeezed her hand. "I am getting out of here soon. I need you to help me, Tempest."

"Anything."

"Baby...get my things. Go to my place and in the bedroom, in my closet you'll find a leather bag. Bring it up here..okay?"

"I don't want to leave you."

"I'll be fine. I only trust you to get these things." It was much easier to talk, and Paul was relieved. When she stood to go, he reached out and placed his hand on her abdomen.

Tempest jumped, his touch made her stomach quiver. A very strange sensation. She saw he was smiling, and placed her hand over his.

He rubbed her stomach, and then seemed to go to sleep.

She left, already anxious to be done and get back to him.

Paul tried to picture his injuries. Mentally, he chanted, I am whole. I am healed. His small voice, his guide, echoed his words. You are whole. You are healed. Warmth suffused his body.

Michael parked his car, and cursed under his breath. So, Tempest thought to cleave to Paul, did she? The little idiot really thought she could dismiss him so easily. He looked up at Paul's building and grinned. Paul, my man. What would I do in your predicament? Cursed, injured.

I'd want my tools of protection with me. And who else would you trust to send, but Tempest? Oh Paul, Love has always been your kinds weakness!

CHAPTER EIGHTEEN

Tempest parked in front of Paul's apartment, opened the manilla envelope the nurse had given her containing his wallet and keys, and ran inside.

When she entered his bedroom, filled with daylight from the open curtains, she was filled with the pleasant memory of the time spent with Paul, sharing, loving.

The bag he wanted was shoved far to the rear of the closet, but she located it and pulled it out. Plopping it on the bed, she noticed a bible on his dresser. Walking over, she picked it up and decided to bring it with her.

Then she felt it, an absence of light. A familiar illness infused her, rank nausea. Michael.

Spinning around she found him standing in the doorway, smiling that cold and detached way of his.

"Tsk, tsk, tsk,...you should have locked the door."

"Why are you here?"

He scanned the room lazily. "I thought we'd share the same taste, Paul and I. Love his decor." He turned his attention back to her. "So tell me. How much do you understand now,..little one?"

There was no way out of the room. Tempest knew she couldn't get past him using force. What was the chance he would just let her go? She doubted he would.

He chuckled, and as if in answer to her unspoken question, stated, "I don't plan to let you out of my sight anymore."

Trembling, she whispered," I've been a fool. I didn't see how foul you are."

Michael actually laughed. "I didn't want you to see anything, so you didn't. Ready to go now?"

"I'm not going anywhere with you." Her stomach rolled with waves of nausea, her head pounded like drums. "I don't want anything to do with you. Not after what you did to Paul!"

Michael took a step closer, his laughter gone. "Don't force me to use painful measures. After all, we work pretty well together, don't we?"

"I hate you!," Tempest gasped, pressing the bible to her chest.

Michael looked at the bible, then at her,..thoughtfully. "Poor, simple, important Tempest. Tell me,..have you finished the books? The ones written by my esteemed, misled teacher?"

Tempest didn't want to have this conversation with him. Paul needed her. She grabbed the bag, still holding the bible close in her other hand, and trying to sound brave, snapped, "I'm leaving."

Michael didn't move. "Oh, Tabor had many things correct. Some things were not supposed to be revealed. I'm sure you were told how he died. But there are some with angel heritage. Or should I say, angelic blood. But that is neither here nor there. Watchers all, but some light and some dark. Yin and yang..you understand. Takes all kinds, my sweet."

Tempest was horrified. Why was he telling her all of this, now? "Who killed tabor Ashe?"

Michael grinned. "Brave girl, to ask me that question. Who ripped him apart? Who sealed his lips? I don't know. I don't think you want to either. But i'll impart something you may not have read yet. It's near the end. There are some with Christ lineage too. The blood line of Jesus. Of Noah. See?
Now why would the church hide something so beautiful in its simplicity?"

She froze. It was too much to absorb. It's impossible.

"Tempest. Do you know you're pregnant?"

Those words motivated her. She almost wanted to laugh. So he could be wrong, like anyone else. "Wrong Michael. I can't have children. Not enough plumbing."

Her words had no effect. He shook his head. "Oh, but you are. You are chosen to have one, actually. A very important one. Your sleeping with Paul changed the odds somewhat, but no matter."

Tempest felt something explode within her. Anger, frustration, she didn't know. "Did you hear me? I can't have kids!!"

Michael rushed forward and attempted to touch her stomach, but she lurched back, dreading his touch. "Have I ever hurt you, Tempest?"

"I want you to just go. Leave me alone! You're crazy!" Without realizing it, she held the bible to her chest. "I'm no Mary, and i'll never be pregnant!"

His face darkened. "Believe what you want, for now. But I will control the child." He stared at the bible. "Look at me Tempest."

She looked at him, those entrancing eyes, but she thought of Paul waiting for her, needing her. Paul hurt,..because of her. The peace and completion she felt in his presence.

Michael broke his gaze, anger all over his face, in his stance.

"Michael, if you don't let me go. I'll hate you forever. I'll never forgive you."

He frowned. "I love you Tempest, don't you know that? I hurt Paul because I couldn't bear to lose you to him. I couldn't bear the thought of you cheating on me, with him!"

She felt the guilt again. She had cheated on him. He had reason to be angry. Her mind swirled with so many things. All the crazy facts

Michael had thrown at her. His supposed love for her. And most overpowering, her need to get to Paul.

"Oh Michael, I was wrong. I understand why you are angry. But Paul isn't the one to be angry with, I am. Please, leave him alone."

Michael clearly saw his mistake. By hurting Paul, he'd made her bond closer to him. How had he miscalculated so badly? It wasn't like him to not think things through. He actually was unsure how to proceed. Did she even realize the bible was protecting her from his influence? And dammit, she was getting stronger! If he took her by force, it would ruin everything. She mustn't be a prisoner. Well, one step back, two forward. It was time to retreat, and reaccess. Taking a deep breath, damn, he hated changing tactics, he stated, "forgive me. I'll remove the curse. As long as Paul leaves me alone, i'll leave him alone. I promise Tempest. Because you asked me to."

"And you'll let me go?" Tempest held her breath, not sure what to expect.

"Go to him. But I'm going to fight to get your love back. I won't lie." He turned and left.

Tempest took a deep, cleansing breath. She grabbed the bag and left the apartment, locking the door behind her. She felt drained...and scared. But Paul needed her so she ran down the stairs to her car, anxious to be there.

Michael watched her drive away, his expression a snarl of pure malice. No one was going to ruin his plans. No one!

During the ride to the hospital, Tempest suffered bouts of shivering, as if a breeze coursed around the back of her neck. Nerves. Michael had shaken her up with his insane speech, talk of Tabor Ashe, and news of her so called pregnancy. Worse, he'd told her he loved her. What was his idea of love?
She had been such a fool, seduced by him, thinking he knew so many secrets and was willing to teach them to her. She wasn't proud of herself. Greed, ego, these things had landed her in this predicament. Wanting to know so much, and thinking herself somehow special. She was stupid, that was all.

The hospital loomed into view and she thought of Paul in his hospital bed. She couldn't wait to be with him..where everything felt right.

Paul basked in the warmth of his body, visualizing organs healing, pulsing with a healthy glow. He touched the bandage covered wound on his chest, felt the heat increase in that area.

A nurse approached the bed and thinking him asleep, clipped a thermometer on his finger. It beeped almost immediately. After a moment, she shook him roughly. "Paul, how do you feel?"

"Good."

"The doctor will be right in to see you. I'm concerned about this fever you're running."

"Don't worry. I'm fine."

She rushed out, writing on the clipboard.

He watched the swaying curtain. Tempest was taking a long time. Was she okay? Time to get out of here.

A doctor came in with the same nurse and took his temperature again. He then checked Paul's pulse, and looked in his eyes. "Are you feeling any pain?"

Paul smiled. "I feel much better."

"Well, we are concerned and need to take a blood sample to check for infection. You have a very high fever."

The doctor removed the dressing from Paul's chest wound. Impossible! It looked like a wound a few months old. He touched the nicely healing suture. How could that be?

Tempest rode the elevator immersed in her thoughts. Should she tell Paul what happened? What Michael had said? How would Paul take all of it? He didn't need any more drama. At the sixth floor, she exited the elevator and walked the sanitary halls to ICU. The curtains to Paul's cubicle were open, and she saw doctors and nurses moving all around him.

He was sitting up, drinking a bottle of water. Seeing her approach, he nodded, smiling. He looked so much better! The swelling was practically gone. Bruising had faded as well. She hesitated to step in with the medical staff so busy with him, but Paul motioned for her to come in.

Standing at his side, Tempest watched the monitors being disconnected. Confused, she heard the excited chatter of nurses.

"I've never seen the likes of it."

"I know. The doctors don't know what to make of it. No one heals that quickly."

"They should run new tests. There has to be an explanation."

"Can't make a patient stay against their will."

Tempest sat the bag on the floor. "Paul. What's going on?"

"I'm getting out of here."

"It's too soon. You're badly hurt."

Paul whispered, "C'mere. Gimme kiss."

For a moment, Tempest thought about the nurses thinking she was his sister, then with a chuckle, planted a deep kiss on his lips. "Now tell me what happened. Seems I can't leave you alone for a second."

"I'm healing really well. I told the docs I want to recuperate at home. Against their wishes, I'm signing out of this joint." He winked at her before turning his attention to some papers a nurse needed him to sign.

Tempest stood in the midst of it all and thought how surreal it was. Fetching Paul's special bag, her altercation with Michael, curses removed, and accelerated healing. She felt her head would explode!

One of the doctors made his disapproval clear. "Paul, you are far from 100 percent. You leave this hospital against our advice."

" I understand, but prefer to recover at home. I'm not comfortable in hospitals."

Inwardly, Tempest laughed at the insanity of it all. The poor hospital staff. The air was abuzz with confusion and interest.

When all the leads were removed, Paul was led to the bathroom to freshen up. Tempest actually giggled when he returned wearing scrubs. Was this the same man who'd died on the table the night before? His strength seemed to be returning rapidly.

Pointing, she teased, "What's with the scrubs?"

He grinned boyishly. "They cut my clothes of when I got here."

Shaking her head, she said, "I'll stay and take care of you. Let's get you home and into bed."

"I'm looking forward to that." He gave her a lecherous look and unable to help herself, Tempest burst out laughing.

Within an hour, they were on their way to Paul's apartment, with many prescriptions to fill, and medical instructions to follow.

Surprising herself, Tempest offered, "Why don't you stay at my place? At least for a few days. I'll take sick days off work and keep an eye on you."

Equally surprised, he asked," are you sure?"

"Very sure. Besides, you have too many stairs at your apartment. We can grab some clothes, then go to my house."

"Tempest,..I love you."

He gave her a look of such depth, that she caught her breath. "I love you too."

Paul affectionately ran his hand down her arm. "When are you going to tell me what happened today. Why it took so long for you to come back?"

Involuntarily, she shivered.

"Oh,..I see. It was Michael."

"Enough about him. Tell me, what's with this miraculous healing? Do you realize the position you put those doctors in, the questions they'll need to answer and rationalize?"

Paul grinned boyishly, and sighed, "Oh, they of little faith."

Tempest couldn't help herself. She burst out laughing.

CHAPTER NINETEEN

The bedroom was thick with smoke and the scent of incense. Michael sat on the edge of the bed. The two women in his bed were resting peacefully. Already, their presence annoyed him.

Rising, he walked to the window and looked out at a beautiful night sky. Stars blinked like tiny diamonds. How did I mess things up so badly? Was I too anxious? What other reason was there for making such a stupid mistake? Damn, I need a new strategy. A soft voice broke his focus.

"Michael, come to bed."

Michael snapped, " Get out you little bitch. Wake your friend, and get out."

"Don't you want to join us for more,..fun?"

Michael's frustration exploded within him. Two steps brought him to the bed where he ripped the sheet up and off the bed, revealing two naked women of exceptional beauty. One had a black eye, the other a bruised cheek and swollen lip. "To have more fun with you two dogs, I'd have to kill you. Now get out of my house before I accept your offer!"

They scrambled off the bed and snatched their clothes from the floor, before silently running out of the room.

When he heard the front door slam shut, Michael walked down to the kitchen and reached for the telephone. It was finally time to report.

Monsignor Clementine Sebastien closed the heavy volume he'd finished reading. He was as angry now as he'd been when he first read this book. Tabor Ashe. Father Ashe, a good friend. Would he ever understand why this man had turned against them? One of their most trusted, and talented. With a weary sigh, he looked at the walls around him. Not really walls actually, but bookshelves of mahogany wood.

They stretched up to meet the high ceiling painted with pictures of vines and grapes. These bookshelves held ancient volumes, as well as new publications. He loved this library. It smelled of lemon polish, and held so many secrets. Very few would ever see the inside of this room,..which was why he spent as much time here as possible.

There was a soft knock at the door. "Enter."

A young man came in wearing a long black robe and large gold cross dangling from his neck. Eyes downcaste, he handed a phone to him. "It is Michael, Monsignor."

"Ahh, thank you."

The man nodded, and left quickly.

Placing the phone to his ear, the Monsignor pleasantly greeted, "Hello Michael. I was beginning to worry. Do you have news?"

Michael sat at the kitchen table and tried to think of the best way to reply. "She is with child Monsignor. She does not know it, but she is. But, I have made an error in judgement and she has broken my hold on her."

After a few moments of total silence, the Monsignor replied, " How is this possible, Michael?"

"What we feared has come to pass. She has acquired a guardian of angelic blood."

"This was not unexpected. Be rid of him."

"I tried. He wasn't allowed to die. And now, knowing I was the reason for his injuries, the woman has bonded with him."

"Michael. I'm surprised by this. You have never been sloppy. Maybe you need help with this matter. The child must be ours to rear, and you put that at great risk."

Michael squeezed the receiver, knowing if he spoke now, he'd say the wrong thing. How dare this minor player call him sloppy? It was their blessing to have his help. Any of their kinds help! Composing himself, he finally replied, "Clementine, You put your trust in me. Tempest,..and her child, will be ours. Give me time."

"Tread lightly Michael."

The line went dead. Michael leaned back in the chair and closed his eyes. Tread lightly huh? How would the great church feel if he took their prize for his own. His alone?

The idea made him chuckle, but there was no mirth in it. More a resolve. Tread lightly indeed.

CHAPTER TWENTY

Standing in her sunlit kitchen, slicing a lemon to put into their tea, Tempest was struck by something. She was happy! The sounds from the livingroom, of Paul using the remote to change channels on the t.v. from his comfortable spot on the couch, the aroma of hot steamy herbal tea with lemon, all made this place feel like home again.

Paul laughed out loud at something on the television and she grinned. The last time she'd felt this happy and complete...well...was when her folks had been alive.

Placing two cups of tea on a tray with scones and butter, she carried it into the livingroom. Paul was stretched out on the couch under a quilt, and smiling from ear to ear. He greeted, "Hey sweetie."

A smile bloomed within her. "Heeey," It came out like a song, yes...happy. She carefully handed him a mug of tea and set the tray on the floor beside him. Then she sat on the end of the couch and placed his feet in her lap. "You comfy?"

"Very," he tickled her with his feet. "So,..are you ready to talk about it now?"

Reluctantly, Tempest nodded. There was only so long that she could avoid telling him what happened at his place, with Michael. All she wanted to do was sit here with Paul, enjoying his company and taking care of him. But she had to tell him, so now was as good a time as any.

Paul set his tea down on the tray and gave her an encouraging look. She studied him. Was it really just a few days ago that she'd almost lost this man? He looked so healthy. It was a miracle!

"Okay. When I went to your apartment to get your bag, I forgot to lock the door, and Michael showed up. He wanted me to go with him. Michael was talking crazy. About bloodlines of angels. Bloodlines of

Christ."

Paul nodded slowly, his face expressionless.

"He spoke about why Tabor Ashe was killed, for revealing secrets,..and, " she took a deep breath, "he insisted I was pregnant! That he would control the child. That I was chosen. I told him I can't have kids, but he wouldn't listen. He said he loved me and because of that, he'd take the curse off of you. He is insane! I was so afraid of him..and he made me feel sick again too. I've been so stupid! I never want to see him again."

Paul sat up and took her hands in his. "Tempest,..he isn't crazy."

"He is!"

"No baby. He isn't. We both, he and I, have Angelic blood. Our ancestors were fallen ones. Ones who took human wives, had children."

Her chest felt tight. "But in the bible, it says the flood was to kill all of them."

"Yes, the great flood was to destroy the monsters that some of these children became. But some were spared. Look at your greek myths. Your fairy tales. Look with new eyes at mankinds fables. All of us were not killed. Bloodlines continued. Many in power know this, but the secret is well kept. Some of our kind have made alliances with those in power. The church, and government."

The tight feeling in Tempests chest increased, and it felt hard to breathe. How could she believe this? It would mean that the world was a huge mystery, and all its occupants were walking around blind, only thinking they could see. She wanted to cry.

Paul squeezed her hand. "It's alright, Tempest. Just listen, and absorb what you can. Okay?"

She nodded, fighting the tears.

Paul continued. "Another side of the coin is that there are those with the bloodline of Jesus. The blood of Mary. Blood chosen by God to flow through his son. You have that blood."

"But,..that's impossible!"

"No, it isn't. You have that blood prized above all others. And you are pregnant. A child with the blood of Angels, and the blood of Christ. A child with the power to bring the fallen ones, and their ancestors, the chance for forgiveness."

"But Paul,..c'mon. How can this be? I'm not worthy to carry such a special child! I can't! And what...why...",she stiffened. "Why is this happening?"

Paul pulled her closer. "Do you trust me?"

"Yes,..but...none of this makes sense to me. And,..I don't think I want it to. I'm scared."

"I know it scares you. But sweetie, you need to know. There's no more time to evaluate things. Don't be afraid. I will protect you and the child to the death. I love you both."

Dizziness hit her like a punch. She couldn't breathe. Hugging him, she desperately tried to get her bearings, but knew she was about to pass out. "I can't breathe."

"Shhh." Paul cupped the back of her head in his hands and kissed her. "Shhh, concentrate on your heartbeat. Think only of that."

She felt the heat of his body infuse hers, and tried to do as he asked. It felt as if a scream was rising through her, trying to break free.

"It's okay, Tempest. Your mind wants to reject all of this...to protect you. But it must open up more than it ever has. Your mind must completely wake up. Don't panic, love. I have you."

As the tears fell, she heard her heart slowing, beating in rythm. Comforting. A baby. Was she really carrying a baby? Her own baby? Crying harder, she hugged Paul close and dared to accept the things he told her. She realized he was singing softly in another tongue, and it sounded like a lullabye. It felt like love.

CHAPTER TWENTY ONE

Monsignor Clementine Sebastian sat on a huge, ornate, gold trimmed chair. He looked like another decoration in the larg room, with his white, gold trimmed robe and cross. The room's walls were blood red, with carved gold moldings. It's domed ceiling was also gold, carved cherubs circling the perimeter.

He wasn't impressed by the lush surroundings. There were more important matters at hand. The large double doors before him opened and three robed men strode in. All three stood at least six feet tall, and were very slender. Their black robes swept the floor. Clearly of varied races, their beauty was exceptional. Two had long, flowing blonde hair. One seemed to be of German descent, the other olive skinned. The third had short cropped bluish black hair, and was obviously asian in appearance. It was he who spoke first.

"Hello, Clementine. What is so urgent that you felt the need to summon us from the coast? Are you aware that we were unable to complete our assignment?" His voice dripped with disdain.

The monsignor tried to hide his dislike of these three. Their sort made him uneasy. Assassins, cleaners. But, his intuition told him they were needed. "I am aware that you were in the midst of some important work. But,I suspect there may be a problem with your brother, Michael Rivendi in Boston."

All three looked at each other.

"Clementine,..is it the child?"

"Yes."

Their expressionless faces seemed to light up from within.

"What must we do?"

The Monsignor smiled and relaxed a bit. Now he had their attention. "For now, I just want you to observe. Michael has admitted making an error which could affect his acquiring this child. The mother has acqired a protector as well."

One of the blondes stepped further into the room. "And who is this protector?"

"He is one protected by Uriel. Paul Carson."

"Ah, Paul. So he has finally chosen his path."

Clementine nodded. "Yes, he's chosen the traitors path."

All three narrowed their eyes, and focused on him intently.
The blonde spoke again, very softly. "No. He is not a traitor. He has just chosen a different path."

Clementine struggled not to squirm under their scrutiny.
He looked at them thoughtfully. Angelo, Sigmud, Chao. Known as The Three. But were they loyal?

They smiled at him and he felt chilled inside. "So,"Chao stated,"we are to observe only?"

"Yes. If Michael cannot do this on his own, aid him. Do not harm the woman, Tempest. That would be very detrimental. Dispose of Paul, if necessary."

They stared at him for what seemed an eternity, then abruptly swung about and left. The scent of roses lingered in the air.

The Monsignor took a shaky breath. Thank goodness that was over!

Tempest walked into the drug store. As she waited for Paul's prescription refills, she noticed the pregnancy tests. Selecting one, she purchased it along with the medicine, and walked outside to her car. She was startled to see Michael standing there. Having no idea what to expect, she turned to go back into the store, and some semblance of safety.

"Tempest. You don't have to run. I'm not a threat anymore."

Something in his voice stopped her. Was the sincere sound in his voice real?

"What are you doing here Michael?"

"I was driving past and noticed your car. I just wanted to see how you were doing?"

As always, she was struck by how handsome he was. But Paul was more beautiful. His beauty was within, as well as without. She smiled and walked to her car."I'm fine, just fine."

"I'm happy to hear that."

She waited, but no nausea. Relieved, she firmly stated,"Michael. I'm with Paul now. I love him."

"I know that. I'm not here to beg you to be with me. I just want to remain your friend. To continue your lessons, if you'd like. I'm willing to speak with Paul and make it clear I'm not any threat."

Tempest was stunned. This wasn't the Michael she knew. He had to be up to something. But what?

"I don't think Paul would feel like seeing you, Michael. I'm sure you understand why."

He smiled at her. Tempest tried to feel his emotions, test his sincerity, but he was a blank page. Nothing.

"Well, Tempest. You look beautiful. Please mention to Paul, that I'd love to see him and apologize. To talk to you both. Perhaps, despite everything, we could call upon our higher good and be friends. One of us is the father of your child. Shouldn't we be close, if only for that reason. The three of us? Think about that, okay?"

He turned and began to walk to his car. "Good seeing you, sweetheart. Pregnancy becomes you."

Tempest got into her car and locked the doors. Was it possible? Had he somehow come to his senses? What would Paul say when she ran all of this by him? Would he forgive Michael? She didn't know what to make of it! This sudden change of heart was hard to swallow.

CHAPTER TWENTY TWO

The sleek, black private jet, landed smoothly at Logan Airport. Within its lush confines, the three prepared to disembark.

Sigmud closed his laptop computer and tucked it under his arm.

Angelo exited the bathroom, a huge logbook in his arms. Chao locked a large briefcase he'd been inspecting.

The pilots voice crackled over the speakers,"You may disembark now. Your limo has arrived."

The exit door opened with the gentle "whoosh," of escaping air pressure. Without a word, they got up and exited the airplane.

The area they were in was secluded although well lit. Before approaching the limo, they carefully scanned the area. Only when it felt safe did they leave the plane's shadow to enter the limo.

Chao broke the silence, and asked the driver, "Where will you take us?"

"I am to take you to Saint Magdalena of the Lost seminary. There you will have lodging and meals. Vehicles will be at your disposal as well."

Satisfied, The Three sat back to enjoy the ride through this new and unfamiliar city.

Paul stood in the doorway, worried. He had been careless. How could he let Tempest talk him into letting her go to the store,alone? It had been a while and she wasn't back yet. And it was dark. And there was more. Something was in the wind,a sense of change. He felt tense. What was different all of a sudden?

Tempest parked the car, and when she got out, immediatly noticed Paul in the doorway. Something must be wrong. Panic gripped her. She rushed up the stairs to hug him. "Are you alright?"

He laughed softly. "I'm great. I was worried about you. Everything okay, no problems?"

She handed him the prescription bag and kissed him."I ran into Michael. Let's go inside and I'll tell you about it."

As they walked inside, Tempest realized Paul had been here with her for an entire week. It had been heaven, and she dreaded returning to work. But he was healing at an exceptional rate, and she had to make a living.

The aroma of tangy spaghetti filled the house. "Don't tell me you cooked?"

Paul winked at her. "Spaghetti and meatballs, my specialty." Once they reached the kitchen, he pulled out a chair. "So, sit and tell me what Michael had to say."

She sat and waited for him to do the same, then told him word for word what Michael had said, watching Paul's face for a response. He only seemed amused.

"So,..he wants friendship and forgiveness. Interesting." Paul grinned. "Do you believe any of it?"

"Not really." She thought about something he'd said. If she was pregnant, who was the father? It was more likely to be Michael than Paul, but not guaranteed. This whole train of thought made her very uncomfortable. "What if he is the father, Paul?"

To her surprise, Paul just shrugged.

"But if by some miracle I'm pregnant, like both of you insist, won't that matter? Paternity?"

Paul frowned coldly. Tempest was stunned by the change in his mood. She had never seen him like this. "Paul?"

He seemed to snap out of his mood. "I'm sorry Tempest. I was thinking. That's all. It really won't matter if he's the father. The child is what matters. Your child needs to be surrounded by what is needed and required for it to be prepared for it's purpose."

Tempest dreaded this conversation. The "it" he discussed so matter of factly would be her child. A bundle of smiles and powdery sweetness. Her baby. What the baby required was her! "Paul, what is required and needed for my baby? What is this childs purpose?"

"You'll understand in time. Trust me."

Oh how she trusted him, and loved him. But for that fleeting moment, when his expression had changed, there hadn't seemed to be much difference between him and Michael.

Paul watched her as she thought these things, with a knowing smile. "Tempest, do you think I should forgive Michael? Do you want to let him in your life again?"

She sighed. "I don't trust him. In a way I think he's sorry he hurt you,but I'm not sure about that. No. I don't want to let him into my life. He frightens me, and I never want to be under his control again."

"Do you think he's the father?"

She looked into Pauls eyes. "I don't even believe I'm pregnant. I bought an at home test, so in the morning, I'll know."

He smiled warmly at her, and nodded. Then Paul got up and fixed their dinner plates, the conversation ended.

Tempest's stomach felt like a tight knot. She felt like she always did after taking any kind of test. Was Paul testing her, and had she passed?

CHAPTER TWENTY THREE

The sound of children's laughter floated on the cool air. Michael leaned against his car outside the park, enjoying the brisk wind. Ah, he so loved fall. There was the hint of rain in the air. At first, standing here enjoying the scenery in the park, and listening to its occupants, had uplifted him. Yet, as always, his mind drifted back to Tempest.

She had closed herself to him. He understood how she'd done it, but wondered if she was aware. Love. Love closed him out. One barrier he couldn't cross or manipulate. Love. The fool actually loved Paul. Worse, just as love closed her to him, it also protected Paul. If he did anything to him, she'd suspect him immediately, and her dislike would become hate!

Damn! He had never made such a huge mistake before. He still couldn't believe he'd allowed his emotions to plunge him into this quandary. There weren't many options open. He could visit Paul and offer fake humility, which Paul would promptly see through, or he could watch and wait. Then, when she was well into her pregnancy, abduct her. The child had to be his, after all. He'd planned everything too damn well!

Michael looked up at the sky, where dark clouds were beginning to roll in. Ancestor, where are you? Have you deserted me? Have I shamed you? He felt nothing. Not the familiar feeling of comfort, the rejuvenating presence of his angelic ancestor. Nothing at all. Only dark clouds in a gray sky, and the hesitant touch of a raindrop.

Angrily, he got in his car and began the drive home. It was really raining now, a heavy downpour. How appropriate, he thought, matches my mood.

As he entered his street, a bad feeling overcame him, dread. A feeling he wasn't used to at all. He parked and before getting out, looked all around his house and shop. There were cars parked as always. Some were unfamiliar but that wasn't unusual. But,..something wasn't right.

Michael grabbed his keys and carefully exited the car. Softly whispering a spell of protection, he quickly walked to the shop and let himself in. His sense of danger increased. Try as he would, he couldn't find the source of his discomfit.

Quietly, he moved up the few steps leading to his shop. When he reached the landing, he froze upon seeing three men standing there. Recognizing them, he understood the dread he'd felt. Michael now felt more than that. He felt fear.

"Are you here to eliminate me?"

The three watched the man before them for a few minutes, expressionless. Angelo strode forward and embraced him. "It has been a long time, brother."

He stepped away and allowed Sigmund and Chao to embrace Michael as well.

Angelo almost smiled as he watched Michael,...almost. "We were asked to watch you, and evaluate how you are handling the current situation. It appears the rift you created with the woman Tempest is too vast for you to cross."

Michael scowled, becoming angry more than fearful. "I told the Monsignor I just needed time."

"No," Angelo corrected, " You need help."

The three formed a half circle around him, as if to prevent any escape. Chao spoke softly. "Your error was arrogance and impatience. A weakness of our kind, is it not?"

Michael nodded, unable to defend himself.

Chao continued calmly, " You underestimated the madonna blood within this Tempest. Love is the power of that bloodline. Love at its purest and simplest. Was not Mary's firstborn a child of pure love,..Jesus? You cannot force this love, you must earn it. How could you forget this, Michael?"

Before he could answer, Sigmud added,"The love this woman is capable of seduced you,..didn't it? She found a way to touch your heart, Michael? You love the woman now, as much as her gift?"

Angelo nodded at Michael, a look strangely like pity on his face.

Michael realized at that moment that he did love her. He was angry at her, he missed her, he desired her, and in his way, he loved her.

Angelo stepped back and allowed Michael to walk further into the room. The three then stood side by side, watching him.

Michael leaned against the counter of his shop, shaken by this revelation. How had he come to love this foolish woman? Looking at them, he pulled himself together as best as he could. They looked unforgiving standing together, dressed immaculatly in dark suits custom fitted to their tall builds. All understood The Three were a force unto themselves. He couldn't afford any mistakes from here on out. "I have never failed before."

Chao nodded solemnly. "That is understood. You are not judged harshly. When the time is right, we will do what is required. Leave the matter in our capable hands."

Michael blurted, "but listen to me...."

He fell silent when they moved closer together and focused their cold gazes on him. When Chao spoke, it was very softly. "You will let this go. It is now out of your hands."

Michael watched them, his heart sinking. They were impenetrable, unbending, fierce. Tempest was lost to him.
Frustrated, he lowered his gaze. Soon he heard them softly descend the stairs and leave.

Tempest looked at the tiny wand in her hand. Paul stood behind her, his hands on her shoulders. "Do you believe me now, sweetie?"

She nodded, unable to tear her eyes away from the bright pink plus sign at the tip of the wand. Smiling, she began to cry, warm in Paul's embrace. She was pregnant. It was a miracle.

CHAPTER TWENTY FOUR

Early morning news reports blasted over the television speakers, and the scent of coffee was just beginning to fade.

Paul stood at the front window and watched Tempest get in her car, and drive away to return to work. He rubbed his arms where the hair stood on end. Something is wrong, he thought, something is coming.

Deciding he needed to go home for a while, he grabbed his coat. He could take care of some chores while she was working, and possibly prepare for whatever was about to go down. Hopefully, he could keep it away from Tempest.

The feeling of dread had started as a tiny inkling that all wasn't right with his world. A prick of unease. But it increased and now it was a constant drain on him. He needed to go home and replenish his center, grab some herbs and vitamins.

Paul locked the door behind him and walked out to his car, which Maggie had been kind enough to retrieve and park there.

The sun was bright overhead, but it gave no heat. The air was frigid. Paul quickly drove home.

There was a black BMW parked in front of his apartments. Right away, the bad feelings increased. Taking a deep breath, he parked behind it. Paul didn't get out right away. Unable to see through the BMW's heavily tinted windows, he took a moment to calm himself. He tried to reason that his nerves were on edge because of everything that had happened, but he knew better. The years had taught him better. Confrontation was inevitable. Tempest is worth stepping back into the arena. The child even more so.

Stepping out of his car, he began walking toward the stairs. The door of the BMW swung open and three extremely tall, well dressed beings stepped out. They stood side by side and called out to him. "Paul,..be still."

Recognizing the authority in their voices, Paul turned to face them. "I am not under the will of the church."

Chao smiled. "You are under a will greater than that of the church."

Paul felt a rush of fear, but fought against it. "That is true. But I have been granted free will,..just as you have."

"Uh uh uh..."Chao grinned. "MAN has been granted free will. You are not truly a man,..are you?"

Fighting the urge to flee, Paul studied the three men. These men emitted power of such strength, that he almost wanted to bow to them. It had to be the ones he'd heard of,..The Three.

The men stepped closer to him. "We need to talk, Paul. You know why this is so."

Paul was at a loss for words. He didn't know what to do.
It was then he heard his inner voice. Something he trusted. Stand your ground. Let them see your commitment. Show no fear. Standing tall, he smiled back at Chao. "I have done nothing wrong. Why were you sent to me?"

"The woman Tempest, and her child. Do you intend to keep them?" Chao's smile vanished. His eyes narrowed. "That is why we were sent to you."

"I love her, and she loves me. The child is hers, and hers alone. She has free will and she alone can choose the fate of her child. I am simply taking care of the ones I love."

Angelo snapped. "Words!"

Chao placed his hand on his chest, and Angelo fell silent. All three studied Paul for a seemingly endless time.

Paul couldn't read them at all. It was fascinating and frightening at the same time. They almost seemed like triplets, although obviously not.

Chao quickly reached out and placed his palm on Paul's heart. There was no warning, no way to move out of reach.

Paul felt a warm current fill his chest, and then the images came. Open blue sky lit by brilliant sun. A lake of burning flame, too hot to bear. White light...more bright than anything he'd ever seen...or remembered. Out of this light came a voice so soothing, he wanted to weep. "I know you."

Then he was grabbing at his chest, but the hand was gone. And so were the three. As if they'd never been there at all!

Disoriented, Paul looked up and down the street. The BMW and its occupants were gone. What had they done to him? The vision confused him even though there was a vague familiarity to it.

Worried about Tempest, he got in his car and drove to her job. Paul's heart was racing, and long buried memories began to surface. Memories of a little boy drawn to the church, because there he didn't feel so different. Holding his grandmothers hand as they walked to church, where she was director of Sunday school.

He met Father Tabor Ashe when he was twelve years old. He was a lonely boy, close only to his grandmother who accepted everything about him. The visions, the voices. It had been a very hot day, so he sat in the cool dark church waiting for his grandmother to finish a meeting upstairs.

A priest entered the church and walked up to the front where he began lighting candles for evening mass. He noticed him sitting alone and asked, "May I help you?"

Paul looked into the kindest eyes he'd ever seen. "I'm waiting for my grandmother."

The priest studied him a moment. Then he motioned with his hand. "Come here. Are you Paul?"

Paul didn't know what to make of him. He felt lots of things from the priest. Excitement. Happiness and relief.
He wasn't sure he wanted to go to this man.

When Paul didn't move, the man smiled. "I'm father Ashe. Tabor Ashe. I was hoping to meet you."

"Why?" Paul knew he was being rude, but he couldn't help it. He felt confused by this priest.

Father Ashe came and sat next to him. "Young one, you can feel my excitement,...can't you?"

Paul nodded.

"Of course. You are a special one. There are others Paul. You aren't alone."

"Special how?" Paul, the child, felt hope.

The priest had laughed. "Seers, knowers, angelic ones. Would you like to know more about yourself?"

Paul began to speak, but a boy around his age with golden hair to his shoulders, entered the church. "Father Ashe, you are needed."

The priest smiled back at the boy and nodded. "Alright Michael. I'll be right there."

Paul grabbed his arm. "Father,...is he like me?"

Father Ashe pat his hand. "We are all individuals,...even your kind."

With that said, he got up and left the church.

When his grandmother came to get him, Paul kept the meeting a secret. Instinctively, he knew that Father Ashe was the one thing she would NOT understand.

Returning to the present, Paul parked a distance from Tempest's job. He didn't see any sign of The Three , and relaxed just a little. He still couldn't believe that he was on their radar now. That he was still breathing! Well, the most he could do was sit right here and keep watch until Tempest left work and safely got into her car.

*   *   *

Tempest sealed the last envelope to be mailed and sighed with relief. Grinning, she realized she hadn't missed this at all.

She wanted to be home with Paul, making baby plans. Just enjoying his company. There was a soft knock at her office door. She quickly smoothed her blouse and skirt before saying," Come in."

Tempest looked up to see three tall, well dressed men enter, and close the door behind them. They were so beautiful to look at that she was stunned. How could all three be so tall? She felt a quick flash of fear because they seemed abnormal somehow. "May I help you?"

Two of them were blonde, one well tanned. One was asian. He was the one who answered her. "Is your name Tempest?"

"Yes. I'm sorry, did we have an appointment?"

He smiled at her. So did the two blondes. Tempest felt repulsed by their smiles. It didn't quite reach their exquisite eyes.

One of the blondes stepped up to her desk. " I am Sigmud, and they are Chao and Angelo."

She pushed her seat back, alarmed. What did they want with her? Protectively, she held her stomach with one hand. Chao's eyes focused there, and his expression softened.

Sigmud soothed, "You don't have to fear us. We only wish the best for you and your child."

Leaping from her seat, Tempest whispered, "What do you want?"

"To make sure that you are protected. To make sure your child is not used in any way."

She stared at them, fighting her rising panic. The two blondes so reminded her of Michael. "Please,...just leave us alone."

Chao motioned to Sigmud to move back from the desk, and was obeyed. He looked at her, his features gentle now.

"We cannot do that Tempest. There is too much at stake. There are many agendas, sweet one. Many agendas. But we know the real truth,...us alone. Don't fear, for we are your protection. Expect us when your time is near. Not with fear,...but with joy."

Quietly, they turned and left.

Tempests heart was beating like a drum. Breathing deeply, she willed herself to calm down. She had never been so afraid. Power seeped from the three men like waves. She sat down and called the house, desperate to tell Paul about what had happened. He would be able to put her mind at ease, he always did. The phone rang and rang.

Where are you Paul?

CHAPTER TWENTY FIVE

Michael lay naked on his bed, eyes closed. He caressed a blue stone in each hand. At first he thought about Tempest, trying to find a way to get to her, and avoid The Three. But his weary mind took another path. The path of childhood memories.

He had been 11 years old when he met Paul. The church was all he knew. An orphan, he was befriended by Father Tabor Ashe, who often gave services to them at their group home. He noticed the thin, quiet blonde child who always came back from foster homes, unwanted. Foster parents were all afraid of the ten year old with the intense gaze far beyond his years. The little boy who would crawl onto the roof, or sneak outside at night to stare up at the sky. Who rarely spoke, but saw too much. They rushed him back to the state, happy to be rid of his uncomfortable presence.

But Father Ashe, he looked at him differently. One day after Mass, he came to his room. "Michael, pack your things. You're leaving today."

Michael remembered how those words made him feel. Sad, lost,..and hopeful all at the same time. Another family would surely reject him. But having no choice, he packed and followed Father Ashe out to his car. As he settled in, the priest had looked at him with his kind eyes, and smiled.

"Well Michael. You can relax now. You can be yourself from now on. You'll live with me and my brethren. There are many like you, and you'll get to meet them now. "

Confused, Michael asked, "Like me?"

"Yes Michael. Gifted with knowing. Able to hear things and make things happen. It's because of your blood."

His blood. Father Ashe confused him. "You know my parents?"

Father Ashe chuckled and started the car. "You are beyond your parents, Michael. Their fate lies in your hands. You have the blood of an angel. That is what matters. And you are no longer alone."

His life began that day. A life full of learning scripture and prophecy, known and unknown. Of learning about himself, and his many abilities. Most importantly of all, he was loved.

After being there for several months, Paul began to visit. A lanky, brown skinned boy with sad eyes, and a mystery about him. Michael liked him instantly. There was something about the way he carried himself. A confidence. They became friends. Father Ashe called them two sides of the same coin, and how they had laughed. They were best friends until right after Paul turned sixteen.

Father Ashe and the others spent more time with Paul because he was a fast learner, and he had an inner voice, his compass within him that he totally trusted. He was a thinker more than a doer. Michael was impetuous, and often scolded.

Sometimes, he felt jealous of the attention Paul received, and he said cruel things. He called Paul soft, or accused him of thinking he was better than all the others. Michael would see the pain his words caused in Paul's eyes, and it pleased him.

Then one day, Father Ashe was called to go to Rome. There was great excitement among the priests. Michael wanted to go so badly! Oh, to see the Vatican, and the elders of his kind. To have the honor of viewing the secret books which told their history.

Using deception, Father Ashe somehow acquired permission from Paul's grandmother to take him with him. Paul was going to Rome!

Michael watched as Paul packed the new robes given to him, and his papers, and he fought his tears. Jealousy consumed him. He had been here first! Father Ashe found him first! It wasn't fair!

As Paul got into the car with Father Ashe and two other priests, to go to the airport, he began to hate his best friend.

The distance between them widened from that day forward, and then one day Paul left. Michael continued his studies. As much as he respected Tabor Ashe, he never forgave him for choosing Paul.

Michael sat up in bed and threw his stones across the room. The fresh pain of his memories filled him, and tears flooded his eyes. Paul, why is it always you? Why? What makes you easier to love?!

His hatred of Paul renewed, he knew he had to gain his trust somehow. But how?

CHAPTER TWENTY SIX

Impatient, and increasingly worried as each minute passed, Paul got out of his car and locked the doors. As he headed for Tempest's workplace, he noticed a black BMW pulling away from the curb, about a block away. How had he missed them? Heart racing, Paul ran, thinking all kinds of horrible things.

Had they taken Tempest away, or worse, killed her? Why had they come to see her, if not to take some kind of action.

He sprinted up the stairs to the fourth floor. The elevator was too slow.

When he entered the reception area, he saw her office door was closed. Without a word to the receptionist, he ran for it, and opened the door.

Tempest locked her desk. She needed to see Paul right away! Only then would she feel safe. Who were those three men? Shivering, she tried to calm herself. Paul needed to tell her everything. She wouldn't take no for an answer. It was time she knew exactly what was going on!

The office door crashed open. Tempest jumped, sure they had come back for her. Desperately, she scanned the office for any kind of weapon.

"Tempest! Are you alright?"

Hearing Paul's voice, she ran to him and hugged him tightly, her heart pounding wildly. Calming down, Tempest noticed some co-workers had congregated around the door. She stepped away from Paul and composed herself. "Everything's okay," she reassured them. "Just a bit of a family emergency."

A few people looked unconvinced, but they all returned to their own workspaces.

Turning her attention back to Paul, she saw worry written all over his face. "You know what happened today, don't you?" His nod confirmed it.

Paul was so relieved to see her breathing, and vibrant. Alive! What would he do if something happened to her? The thought was too horrible to conceive!

Tempest looked into his dark, serious eyes, and all her fear drained away.

"We're leaving here, and you are going to tell me everything. All of it. Okay Paul?"

His reply was to pull her into a tight embrace, and just hold her. Just listen to the steady beat of her heart, and feel her soft curves fit to his. Just hold her. "let's get out of here, babe. I'll tell you everything you want to know."

Paul offered to make Tempest something to eat, and left her resting on the couch. While he put water on for tea, he recalled what she'd told him about her visit from The Three. No wonder she was terrified. He couldn't understand why they had told her they wanted to protect her and the baby. It didn't make sense. He knew they were under the control of the church. The idea that they would go against the church,..well, it was inconceivable! Michael, The Three,..all wanting possession of Tempest. Like so many times before, he remembered a trip long ago, taken with Father Tabor Ashe. It spelled the end of his close friendship with

Michael. He also learned of the salvation to come.

The Child of Chance. The last chance of forgiveness for the fallen ones, and their offspring, the Nephilim.

He made two caesar salads, and lowered his head. Tempest would need some sustenance. Her world was about to change drastically. Paul wasn't sure she would be able to accept it. Really, she had no choice. Just as he'd had no choice.

He was 17 when he took that fateful trip. How excited he had been. He was going to Rome! To the Vatican!! And he was to have an audience with the Pope! Father Tabor Ashe had insisted on his accompanying him. There were secret meetings among all the priests, and long distance calls. All of this served to excite his young mind even more. Not only had he found others who were just like him, and able to teach him so much, but he had actually found favor among them!

The trip was like a dream. Paul was dressed like the priests he accompanied. A long, gold trimmed robe and sash. A wooden cross on a silver chain dangled around his neck. He sat next to Father Ashe in a limo, which drove them to the airport. During the long flight, Paul was told to study.

Huge, aged volumes were given to him to read, and remember. Books which told of great sin, and punishment. Destruction and desire. Broken rules,..and giants of great reknown. He had read them, and strangely, he'd remembered things. Flames, bright light.

When they entered the Vatican, his eyes were dazzled, and his mind overcome. Such wealth and grandeur at every turn! And they were treated like royalty. After days of being stared at by everyone, or actually touched, Paul felt somewhat like an animal in the zoo. "Blood of Danel," they whispered.
"Angelic blood, blood of the fallen."

Yes, Paul had known of his Angelic heritage, but now he knew the name of his ancestor. Danel. One of the fallen angels who had married and had children with a human wife. One who had disobeyed God's orders. He, and all like him were doomed, because of what their ancestors had done. And then,the day before they left, he was allowed to see, and hold,..the scroll. It was then that his life changed. His very soul changed. And he knew what hope was! There was also an Angel who watched over him!

Breathing deep and steady, Paul pulled away from his memories. There was a task he had to endure in the here and now. He had to make Tempest understand what he barely understood himself. He had to protect her from others who had their own agendas. Bad ones.

Placing lunch on a tray, he went to join Tempest on the couch, and begin a story that would change her view of the world forever.

CHAPTER TWENTY SEVEN

When Paul entered the room, Tempest sat straight, suddenly nervous. He looked so serious. There was sorrow in his eyes. She'd never seen him like this before. When he placed the tray on the floor in front of the couch, she reached out and grasped his hand. "We'll be alright Paul,"she reassured him.

"We handled Michael, and we can handle anything else that comes our way."

Squeezing her hand, he replied,"Eat. I have to get some important things from my apartment, and I'll be right back. Then we will have a long talk."

When Paul mentioned his apartment, it reminded her of his accident. His recovery was miraculous. That was the only way to describe it. Shouldn't she be concerned about that? The doctors sure were. She shivered involuntarily.

Tempest hated having him out of her sight.

"Hurry back."

"Don't worry. I placed protective safeguards on your place when I started staying here." He smiled, but it didn't reach his eyes. They were still sad.

"Paul, you know I love you, right?"

"And I love you. Be right back."

He left before she could say anything else. Tempest stood up to watch from the window as he got in his car. Did she really want to know everything? She wasn't sure anymore.

*   *   *

Paul walked into his bedroom. Funny how his apartment didn't feel like home anymore. He opened the secret compartment in his dresser drawer, and retrieved his papers. He rubbed his hands lovingly over the picture of Uriel,
then pulled a large wooden case from beneath the bed, and hoisted it on top of it. Okay,..now they could have that talk.

Michael parked in front of Tempests' house. He was happy to see that Paul wasn't around, but he could feel all the protections in place. Damn! Seems he wasn't the only one who'd been busy all of these years. Why had Paul hidden his power all this time? Unconsciously, Michael wiggled his healed wrist. What had made Paul run away after his trip to Rome? Not enough love and adoration? He doubted that! The good thing about it all was that once Paul was gone, Tabor had given all his attention to him again. Fickle, weak and stupid Tabor Ashe. Anger curled in Michael's gut like a vengeful serpent. To thrust thoughts of Tabor out of his mind, he tried to sense Tempest within the house, and hear her thoughts. He concentrated so hard that he failed to hear the car parking behind him, it's lights off.

Three hard taps on his window broke Michael's unsuccessful attempts.

He rolled the window down, and Paul peered in at him. The anger returned threefold. Paul just smiled at him.

"Looking for something,..or someone?"

Forcing himself to appear civil, Michael smiled back. "I intended to apologize to you both, but, well...I wasn't sure either of you would see me."

"Try again."

"Alright. It's more than likely Tempest is carrying my child. I want to be in it's life."

Paul laughed softly, before blurting, "Don't pretend you don't know what this child is, Michael. That's all you care about."

"And you don't? You don't want salvation?"

"I want her," Paul snapped. "The rest is gravy."

Michael stared at him as if he were insane. "The rest is gravy?"

Paul turned to leave, but halted as Michael snapped,"of course you want her, you naive imbecile! The blood that flows in that woman makes it impossible not to. At least to our kind. The blood of the holiest of holies,purest of pure, and chosen! I want her too! But since I can't have her, that child, my child, well I have rights."

Angry now, Paul stated coldly, "The only rights you have at this moment, is the right to drive away,...alive."

Michael was chilled. He had never seen an angry Paul, and suddenly, he didn't want to! He hurled desperately, "Do you really think that baby is yours?"

Paul turned to get his things from his car, smiling now. "Does it really matter?"

CHAPTER TWENTY EIGHT

Hearing the front door open, Tempest got up to greet Paul. She felt groggy, having fell asleep. Giving him a big, welcoming kiss, she sighed,"Took you long enough."

"Sorry. Got a little tied up." Paul winked at her. "Did you eat?"

"Yes, but your food is ruined."

"No problem, sweetie."

Tempest looked into his eyes. Something lurked there, but as usual, she couldn't discern what it was. "What tied you up?"

He looked away. "Nothing important."

She began to doubt again. "We don't have to talk tonight. Another time is fine..."

"No, it isn't".

Paul carried the heavy chest and papers into the bedroom. "C'mon."

She followed and leaned against the wall, watching him. When he opened the chest, her innate curiousity took over, and she went to stand next to him. In the chest were very aged books, ornate but old scrolls, some kind of tablets, and stones of many hues. There were some things she didn't even know how to identify. Dried plants maybe? And many pictures.

Among the sheaf of papers he spread at the end of the bed, was a beautiful reproduction of the picture that hung in his livingroom. The Archangel. Some kind of script surrounded it. She dared to reach out and touch it. Her fingers began to tingle. Paul kissed her neck, making her entire body tingle. Tempest had wanted him all day, and now it was getting worse. She wanted him right now.

Paul stopped what he was doing to pull her tight against him. "Stop it,"he whispered against her neck,"behave. Stop trying to sidetrack me."

"I just want you," she whispered back, caressing his arm, loving the feel of his smooth muscle.

With a moan, he stepped back from her. "If I don't do this now, I won't be able to, at all. No matter how much I want to throw you on this bed,..I have to tell you so much. After, you might not want me anymore. I have to give you that choice, after knowing everything."

Taking her face in his hands, Paul bent to look directly into her eyes. "I'm open now. See what you're doing to me?"

For the first time, Tempest could read him! It was amazing. It was as if he was full of colors, his feelings swirling with more intensity than she had ever felt before. He desired her with almost an animal need. She could see all the things he wanted to do to her, and tempest grinned at him, stunned. Deeper than that intense desire, another emotion stirred. Fear. He was afraid he'd lose her. Near tears, she kissed him deeply.

How had she ever thought she loved Michael? He was cruel, and impatient. Not half the man Paul was. Tempest gently tugged some of his soft curls and told him, "Don't be afraid. I can't imagine not loving you. It's not possible for you to frighten or disappoint me."

He didn't seem convinced, which scared her. What was she about to learn?

Paul sat on the bed, and pulled her down beside him. He wasn't quite sure how to begin. "Tempest,..there is a reason why you are going through all of this. It's going to sound far fetched, and crazy, but do you trust me?"
She nodded.

"I met Michael when I was young. We belonged to the same church.

Tabor Ashe, was then Father Tabor Ashe. It was his congregation. He is the one who told me who and what I am. What Michael is. He explained why I didn't fit in, and saw the world in a different way." Paul reached into the box and pulled out one of the books. He opened it to a scripture and handed it to her.

"This helps explain." Tempest began to read, her chest tightening.

GENESIS 6:1 When men began to increase on earth and daughters were born to them, 2 the divine beings [beney ha'elohim] saw how beautiful the daughters of men were and took wives from among those that pleased them. 3 The LORD said, "My breath shall not abide in man forever, since he too is flesh; let the days allowed him be one hundred and twenty years." 4 It was then, and later too, that the Nephilim appeared on earth when the divine beings [beney ha'elohim] cohabited with the daughters of men, who bore them offspring. They were the heroes of old, the men of renown.

Confused, Tempest looked over at Paul to ask a question. He silently handed her another volume, opened to read. She took it, her hand shaking.

1. Then addressing me, He spoke and said Hear, neither be afraid, O righteous Enoch, thou scribe of righteousness: approach hither, and hear

my voice. Go, say to the Watchers of heaven, who have sent thee to pray for them, You ought to pray for men, and not men for you.

2. Wherefore have you forsaken the lofty and holy heaven, which endures for ever, and have lain with women; have defiled yourselves with the daughters of men; have taken to yourselves wives; have acted like the sons of the earth, and have begotten an impious offspring?

3. You being spiritual, holy, and possessing a life which is eternal, have polluted yourselves with women; have begotten in carnal blood; have lusted in the blood of men; and have done as those who are flesh and blood do.

4. These however die and perish.

5. Therefore have I given to them wives, that they might cohabit with them; that sons might be born of them; and that this might be transacted upon earth.

6. But you from the beginning were made spiritual, possessing a life which is eternal, and not subject to death for ever.

7. Therefore I made not wives for you, because, being spiritual, your dwelling is in heaven.

8. Now the giants, who have been born of spirit and of flesh, shall be called upon earth evil spirits, and on earth shall be their habitation. Evil spirits shall proceed from their flesh, because they were Created from above; from the holy Watchers was their beginning and primary foundation. Evil spirits shall they be upon earth, and the spirits of the

wicked shall they be called. The habitation of the spirits of heaven shall be in heaven; but upon earth shall be the habitation of terrestrial spirits, who are born on earth.

Tempest looked at Paul, not really understanding why she should read all of this scripture. Why was he so afraid? Hadn't Tabor Ashe written of some of this? He nodded for her to continue, so she did.

9. The spirits of the giants shall be like clouds, which shall oppress, corrupt, fall, contend, and bruise upon earth.
10. They shall cause lamentation. No food shall they eat; and they shall be thirsty; they shall be concealed, and shall not rise up against the sons of men, and against women; for they come forth during the days of slaughter and destruction.

Stunned, Tempest closed the book. She tried to absorb what she'd read, to make sense of it all. Angels had slept with human women, and had wicked children? They were cursed for eternity?

Paul spoke, his voice raw. "They were the "fallen angels", Tempest. They, and none of their offspring, can ever be forgiven. They constantly beseech, but no..."

She stared at Paul, her gentle Paul. "What does all of this mean? How does it pertain to us?" Holding her breath, she waited for his reply.

Paul couldn't bear to look at her frightened expression, so he stared across the room. "I share their blood, and their punishment. I am a descendant of one of those fallen Angels,..Danel. One of the leaders. Although the great flood killed most of the nephilim, or children of the fallen, some survived.
Me, Michael,..and others, share the bloodlines of these survivors."

"But Paul! You are the gentlest, sweetest man I've ever known!"

He looked at her and smiled sadly."And my long ago ancestor disobeyed Yahweh, and sinned on the earth, and taught humans how to do forbidden things, like make shields, and weapons. And magic. His curse is my curse."

Tempest stood up and shook the book at him. "I don't believe this! It's insane. I won't believe it!"

Paul took the book from her and replaced it in the box. "I went to Rome, the Vatican, at the tender age of 17, and it was then that a circle of elders, very highly ranked clergy, revealed it to me. They showed me their records, where they keep track of all Angelic relations. They are thorough.
Many of our kind serves them. And they told me..other things as well. Things that gave me hope. I learned that one called Uriel saw worth in me...talks to me."

He actually smiled at her. "They told me about you,..the little girl I'd seen in my lonely youth. You."

Tempest sat back down, more afraid than she'd ever been in her life.

"Paul, please,..I don't want to know."

CHAPTER TWENTY NINE

Tempest closed her eyes, suffering the beginning of a sharp headache. And she was confused. It felt like she was immersed in a psychedelic nightmare of horrible proportions! Wake up,..wake up! Then she could make some sense of all of this. Surely, Paul didn't really believe he was a relative of some fictional fallen angel. What were they called,..nephilim? He had to be playing with her head, that was it. But why? Why would a man who claimed to love her, do such a thing?! Why hadn't he told her before, that he grew up with Michael? Stealing a glimpse at him, Tempest began to think he was crazy. Or at least, very delusional. What did he want to tell her now? That she too was angel blood, or worse? Breathing shakily, Tempest was afraid she would pass out. A heavy weariness overcame her. All the things he'd told her before swirled in her consciousness like a poison. How much more was she supposed to accept? She was trying so hard, but this thing about condemnation was too much!

Paul rubbed her back, whispering, "Fight it honey, your mind is trying to shut down. You're kind of in shock, I think."

Sweet, loving, protective Paul was crazy, and Tempest wanted to cry. If this was shock, so be it. Then she was in shock. The man she loved was crazy.

Paul laughed softly, still caressing her. "I'm not crazy. You know that."

Tempest stood up and began to pace, needing to put distance between them.

Her mind was racing, trying to make sense of all she read, and was told. Finally stopping to stand before Paul, she tried to read his face, his eyes. Nothing revealed deceit of any kind. He believed what he told her.

"Are you going to let me finish." He was smiling at her in a patient manner.

"I'm worried about you, Paul."

"Well thank you." He chuckled again."Can I continue now? Are you ready?"

"I'm not joking!!" Tempest took a deep breath, determined to remain rational. "I think you need help."

Paul stared at her thoughtfully before stating,"I won't deny that. But not the kind of help you mean." Grasping her hand, he gently tugged her back to the bed, smoothly forcing her to sit next to him. "I can see you aren't ready to know your role in all of this, just yet. Ask me anything you want to know."

Tempest ran her hand through her hair, and took a deep, refreshing breath. Alright. Paul had asked her to trust him, so let's see how far he'd go.

"Why didn't you tell me you knew Michael?"

"I hadn't seen or spoken to him in years. We weren't on good terms, and I had no real idea of who he was, anymore."

Tempest had to smirk. Nice twisting of words. "Okay then,what exactly did these supposed angels do, when they saw, and slept with women. I mean, what was so bad, that it deserved eternal torment?"

Paul grew very solemn. "Number one, they disobeyed direct orders from God. They were supposed to be watchers, watching over and guiding mankind, but not interfering in their development. But a group of them saw the women were beautiful, and they made a pact, on the summit of Mt. Hermon, to sleep with women, and marry them, and interfere. To disobey direct orders. Huge no no!"

"I understand, but there was mention of teaching mankind things.."

"Yes. The leader, Semjaza, taught how to use charms and enchantments. How to use roots and plants. How to make swords, knives and shields and breastplates. How to use metals of the earth to make jewelry, and the use of make-up. Baraquijal taught astrology. Kokabel taught the constellations. Ezeqeel, the clouds, and Araquiel, earth signs.

And so forth. Things mankind was not meant to know."

Tempest processed all of this. The only use for weapons and armor, was war. Killing. She could see how that was not good. Jewelry and make-up was vanity, and ways to entice. Okay, got that. The other things could cause problems too, especially if used the wrong way, to hurt and harm. In a way, it all made sense. God would not tolerate anyone messing up his plans, who would?

"But why punish their children?"

"They were violent, charismatic, selfish, strong, huge. They were corrupt, probably because no one would dare tell them what to do. These children did all kinds of forbidden things. Understand, Yahweh didn't just punish them. He sent the flood and punished everyone and everything!"

Paul fell silent, as if a veil of sadness descended upon him. Tempest saw the sheen of tears in his eyes. Good Lord! Paul wasn't crazy. This was the truth. How could she possibly doubt him? No wonder he healed so fast! It explained the incredible power Michael had as well. But the two men were different as night and day. How could they share the same fate?

Answering her unasked questions, Paul murmured, "There is no salvation for us. No eternal life. No resurrection. No hope. We can try to live a good and honest life, but it makes no difference. Our blood is bad.

Some of us don't even try to live good. They become bitter, and give in to that bad blood. They lose hope."

Tempest placed her hands around her still flat stomach, and thought of the life growing inside. Another Miracle. An impossibility made possible. Yet, her child, the baby she loved and wanted more than anything, would be cursed with bad blood. Her miracle would be tarnished, without hope. Just like Paul, and Michael. She sobbed, her heart breaking into a million pieces. "Not my baby,"she gasped, barely able to breathe. "Paul,are you letting me know my baby is doomed!?"

Paul pulled her into his lap, and rocked her as she cried. He kissed her hair, her forehead, her face. "Sshh...don't cry. You are so wrong. So wrong."

CHAPTER THIRTY

The library offered little solace. Monsignor Sebastian was too worried to find peace in its books tonight. Why hadn't The Three made contact? And it was time for Michael to call. He did not like being out of contact with them. There was so much at stake, and he knew next to nothing. His contacts at the Vatican were highly agitated. He was unsure of what to do next. If he sent someone to contact the woman, or Paul, there was a good chance they would flee.

Trusting Michael to keep tabs on them was the best course of action, at this juncture. He just wished he'd call!

Michael lay atop his bed, curled in a fetal position. He could feel her! He felt Tempest's distress! Tears filled his eyes. Angrily, he wiped them away.

What kind of trickery was this? How could he feel her at all, protected as she was. But there was no denying it. She was in mental pain, and so afraid! Her emotions battered at him like hammers. What was that idiot, Paul, doing to her!?

Leaping out of bed, he grabbed his car keys from the dresser, and ran downstairs. He had to get to her.

The beat of his heart was comforting. The warmth of his skin soothed her.

Tempest snuggled against Pauls bare chest, and let him hold her in his arms. When she wouldn't stop shaking, he'd removed his clothing, and then hers. She simply let him, weak, and tired from crying. Paul then lay down and held her, until her tears subsided. He was singing to her. Soft, and gentle, words she couldn't understand. But they calmed her spirit. The pitch of the words was odd, but her sorrow drained away. His leg tucked between hers, and his arms wrapped tightly around her, he let her have her cry. And he sang that strange melody of his.

She loved his smell. She loved the way he just held her to comfort, without initiating anything else. She just loved this man. How could he have no hope?

"Paul?" She looked up at his face, and saw such love in his eyes. Such a wealth of concern. "What am I?"

He pulled her even closer."You are not what I am. Your bloodline takes another path. To Jesus. To Mary. After Jesus, Mary had other children. They had children, and so on. That is your bloodline. The bloodline of Gods most beloved. We learned that a time would come, when a woman of holy of holiest blood, would love one like us. And this woman would be gifted and kind. She would bear a child, and this child could find favor with the Most High, and he would end the curse on angelkind. We would have the chance to be redeemed. The Child of Chance. That is who you carry, my love."

Tempest ran a hand down the side of his face, traced his mouth with her finger, then kissed him. "I am carrying the one who could deliver your salvation?"

"Yes. To me, and all that are like me."

She smiled brilliantly. "I'm glad."

Paul rolled atop her, kissing her deeply. As he trailed kisses between her breasts, she whispered, "What were you singing to me?"

"My language." He kissed a breast, then cupped it in his hand. Tempest pressed up against him, wanting him with her entire being. "Angelsong," she sighed, as he opened her legs with his own. She felt his readiness as he pressed against her, willing her to open to him. Grabbing his hips, she rose up to him, sighing as his hardness filled her.

Paul began a slow rythm, watching the emotions play across her face. He could watch this forever, feel this forever. Completion. "Are you mine?"

Tempest moved against him, picking up the pace, her entire body on fire.
"Yes. Yes, always!"

She cried out as he rammed into her with barely controlled violence, branding her, owning her, carrying her to peaks she had never imagined. He brought her to the brink, let her take control, then brought her to the brink again, until they exploded together, fiercely. They fell asleep, joined as one.

Michael stood on the sidewalk, staring up at Tempest's house. The feelings which assailed him were gone. All felt still. For a while, he felt like a small boy again, the boy hungry for love and acceptance. Soon, the feeling was replaced with anger and resentment. What a fool he was, thinking she needed him to rescue her. Paul wouldn't be with her always, and he'd get his chance! He was angry with himself most of all. What was wrong, why couldn't he control his emotions?

CHAPTER THIRTY ONE

The Clinic was crowded, although it was seven in the morning.
Bright sunlight filled the room. Childrens' artwork adorned the pristine,
white walls. Tempest sat next to Paul, his hand clasped in her lap. She
had to be sure. It was time for a pregnancy test.
For three days, she had stayed home with him, learning all about his
youth, and reading a replica of the scroll, which told of the the Child of
Chance. Paul told her it had been found in Egypt, in 1951. The Catholic
church obtained it soon thereafter.

   She finished Tabor Ashe's two books. He revealed the church's plans
for the Child, and it angered her. Tempest had no intention of giving
them any access to her baby!

   When her name was called, she hesitated, actually afraid she wouldn't
be pregnant. Paul kissed her. "Go on. It's all good."

She had blood drawn, urine taken. Then she was examined. Very thorough. Tempest had told them she wanted to be absolutely sure. The nurse told her to return to the waiting area, and that it wouldn't take long. They were all so pleasant and relaxed, but she felt like a coil about to spring.

Paul was still seated, waiting for her. Sitting next to him, she laughed nervously. "Nothing to do now, but wait."

Leaning close, Paul whispered, "Then we can go home and celebrate." That sure redirected her thoughts!

Michael parked around the corner from Paul and Tempest. His urge to stay parked near her house all night had paid off! When he saw them leave the house so early, he'd thought it a good idea to follow them. Maybe he'd have a chance to speak to Tempest, alone. But the reward was even better. Information!

Getting out of his car, he walked to the building they went into. The Templeton Women's Clinic. He fought against going in and demanding to know what they were there for. It was hard, but he managed to turn around and return to his car. Questions flooded his mind. Was the baby alright? Was she pregnant? Worst of all, did she plan to get rid of it? "No," he said aloud, "even Paul wouldn't allow that." The best thing to do now, was to call the Monsignor, and tell him who handled her medical needs. Hopefully, he could find out all they needed to know. He grabbed his cellphone, and quickly placed the call.

Monsignor Clementine Sebastian looked up from his morning ablutions, upon hearing the approach of his acolyte. Noticing the phone in his hand, he smiled hopefully. Taking it, he thanked the young man, and sent him on his way.

"Hello?"

"Monsignor, it's Michael. I have some info you may find useful."

Clementine refrained from scolding him. Instead, he asked, "What information?"

"Accompanied by Paul, she went to a women's clinic. I'm hoping you'll have some connections with the place, and can find out why."

"What is the name of this clinic?"

"Templeton Women's Clinic. It's located in Cambridge, MA."

The Monsignor nodded. "I'll get right on this. Now, have you made any progress with her?"

Michael sounded exasperated. "Not really. Paul stays glued to her side, and he isn't inclined to help my case, as I'm sure you know. I won't give up."

"Get rid of him, Michael!" The Monsignor couldn't be calm anymore. Paul was always a thorn in their side!

"I can't! That's how I lost her, by hurting Paul. If something happens to him, there will be no way at all of influencing her. None."

"Alright,..alright." Clementine kissed the crucifix which hung on his neck, and prayed for patience. "I will let you know if I find anything out. Maybe it will help you somehow."

He hung up as Michael thanked him. It was true that plans had taken a difficult turn, but at least Michael seemed to need him again. Some of his cockiness was gone, thank goodness. Now, to get access to Templeton's womens clinic. They needed to know what was in her records. The more they knew about her, the better!

A nurse came out and called Tempest's name. She got up, motioning for Paul to accompany her. Together, they followed the nurse to a small office, where they were told to wait. Soon, Doctor Samuels came in to talk to them.
Tempest liked his eyes. They were kind. It was one of the reasons she'd picked him as her physician. "Well," he began, sitting at his desk. "You are indeed pregnant."

When he focused on her, Tempest could feel his surprise and confusion. She almost wanted to laugh.

He continued,"I don't understand. Your case is baffling. I know you were told why you can't have children, yet, you are pregnant. It's early, a month at most, but you are pregnant, no doubt about it. "He grinned at her. "I'm almost inclined to call this a miracle." After glancing at Paul, he ventured,

"I hope this is good news."

Tempest smiled, finally accepting it totally. "Is everything alright with the baby?"

"Oh yes. Everything is fine. I will give you a prescription for vitamins, and schedule an appointment for an ultra sound for next week. Alrighty?"

"Thank you, Doctor Samuels." Paul reached out and shook his hand.

"Don't thank me. This has made my day." He grinned at Tempest. "You, take it easy. I'll see you next week."

Paul parked in front of Tempest's house, his heart racing. There was a black BMW parked there. What should he do? He looked over at Tempest, but she didn't seem alarmed at all. Of course not, she didn't know who was near. "Tempest. It's The Three."

Alert, she peered outside, noticing the strange car in front of them. Just then, her front door opened. No one appeared, but the door remained open, as if daring them to come in. "This is my home," she snapped. "I'm not about to run from my own home."

"You don't understand. They're Master Assassins. I don't trust them." All of a sudden, a sense of peace flowed over Paul. His inner voice filled his mind."It's alright. She is protected."

Tempest ended his inner battle by opening the car door and getting out.

"I'm going inside and hear what they have to say."

Paul entered first, his hand holding Tempest back. The house was silent. His protections obviously had no affect on these three. That was disturbing.

A voice called out from the livingroom area, "Paul, enough. We mean you no harm."

Hearing them, Tempest stepped in to stand at his side. She pushed the door closed, then smiled reassuringly at Paul. "We're together. So we'll be okay."

He wished he could be as sure about that.

Tempest walked into the livingroom, trying to seem as brave as possible. The Three stood by the front windows, as impressive as she remembered. They stood six feet tall, or taller. And their beauty was impossible to describe. She could swear she saw light radiate from them. Together, they bowed to her.

Embarrassed, she murmured, "Stop that."

One of the blondes stepped forward. "I am Sigmud." He motioned to the others. "These are my brothers, Angelo, and Chao. We are here because you need us."

Paul was stunned! They wanted to offer aid? But, that meant defying the big boys! He looked at them, trying to notice any signs of deception.

Chao directed his attention to him. "Paul, you have caused some problems, over the years. The Church is quite displeased with you. You have led so many of our kind away from their,..slavery." Chao smiled wide. "We, The Three, have secretly guarded you. We are quite proud of you. You have not lost hope."

Tempest grinned at Paul, loving the total look of shock, and disbelief, on his face.

She wondered, did the church send them to her? Were they really going to go against that great institution?

"Yes." Sigmud smiled at her, tenderly. "The Monsignor sent us to keep things under control. To assure that Michael makes you follow the plan. That plan is to corrupt you, so that our kind can have no chance of forgiveness. They do not think we deserve it. And also, they want to take the child, and incorporate it into the church, as a way of finding more favor for themselves, with Yahweh."

The olive skinned Angelo interrupted. "Are we done now? We must tell her our plans."

Chao gave him a warning look. "Do not mind Angelo. He possesses very little patience. He is more to the point."

"And that point is?" Paul stepped protectively in front of Tempest, facing the three men.

"We know that you love her," Chao stated blandly. "Therefore, we will excuse your rudeness. The point is that Michael found out where

Tempests' doctor is. The Monsignor is obtaining her medical records, even as we speak. This makes the existence of the Child of Chance concrete, and they may move at any time to obtain it. We intend to move you to safety, and protect you until it's birth."

"And after," Angelo added.

CHAPTER THIRTY TWO

Tempest sat comfortably with Angelo, Chao, and Sigmud, poring over a collection of maps and paperwork. The Three had done so much. There were passports. She couldn't believe they already had their pictures in them. It felt weird, knowing that she and Paul had been so exposed. They had properties in Arizona, France, and the Caribbean. Vehicles of all kinds stored at each property. Bank accounts set up, waiting for her. It was overwhelming. Paul studied the passports for awhile, then got up and went into the bedroom.

She asked Sigmud, who sat closest to her, "How long did all of this take? When did you begin planning?"

"We began the moment we learned of the Scroll and all it contained. Our hope was that you would be found in our lifetime, and that we could activate our plans. If not, there were others we would pass the information onto. We do not act alone."

Tempest hesitated to ask her next question, but she had to. "What if the prophesy is false? And I am just a normal pregnant woman, destined to have an average human child? I don't understand how all of you are so sure."

Angelo snapped, "All of the signs were there. Earth events you wouldn't understand, as well as cosmic events. There is no error. Even the Vatican has authenticated this. Why do you think they disposed of your parents? To make you vulnerable. To make you dare to explore your gifts."

Dispose of her parents? Tempest stiffened, holding her breath and trying not to scream. The Vatican had ordered her parents deaths! No!!

Paul locked the door. Carefully, he lay his ancestors picture out, and sat close to it. He needed to know what path to take. Where The Three were concerned, he didn't trust his inner voice to discern right, or wrong. They were too highly trained in the art of deception. Tempests blood seemed to openly welcome them, but he wasn't completely sure. He began to recite the familiar chants that called his ancestor, that woke their connection. The room filled with color and light, and he asked what he needed to know.

Paul returned to the livingroom to find Tempest in a stupor. The Three hovered around her. Sigmud and Chao were scolding Angelo harshly. "You must learn to think before you speak! How many times have you put us in jeopardy with your quick lips? Look what you have done!"

"Exactly what did you do?!" Paul ran to her, and hugged her tight. "Well?"

Angelo admitted, "I had no ill intention. I thought she had put two and two together. She did not know the Vatican disposed of her parents."

Paul wanted to strangle him! He had his own suspicions about her parents, and his being abandoned as a child at the hospital, for that matter! Why couldn't Angelo keep his big mouth shut!?

"My blood came from them," Tempest mumbled, "Why kill them?" Michael knew the answer to her question. They were minor, and she was the prize. His heart broke for her. The deep sorrow she felt infused him. For once, he didn't know how to comfort her.

Chao turned to Paul. "We will erase this knowledge from her mind. It isn't good for her to lament like this."

Horrified, Paul jumped in front of her. "You don't have that right!"

Chao frowned, and looked past him at Tempest. "We can take this knowledge from you. What is your wish?"

Knowing that her parents were murdered was so painful, Tempest actually considered not knowing. But she also realized, knowing would keep her anger unsullied. "I don't want to forget." She pushed the papers away, and ran to the bedroom, slamming the door.

Michael drove past Tempest's house, shocked. A black BMW! Oh shit! The Three were there. He drove slowly, not sure what to make of it. He had decided to keep an eye on her, just to stay aware of her coming and goings, but this was completely unexpected. What did they want with her at this time? It didn't make sense. He made a decision, and parked. It was going to be painful, but he had to walk through that invisible bubble of protection Paul had so carefully constructed, and ring the bell. He had to know what the hell was going on!

The Three moved together fluidly, standing side by side, and looked at Paul,hard. "Michael is here. He is coming to the door."

Paul quickly gathered all the paperwork, and took it into the bedroom, where Tempest sat on the bed, staring into space.

She looked up at him and nodded. "I know. Michael is here."

Just then the doorbell rang.

Michael wanted to scream out in agony. The banging in his head was too intense. It took all of his will to withstand it. And his heart, it was beating too fast. Paul, how he'd underestimated him! He lay on the bell, struggling to stay on his feet.

To his surprise, it was Tempest who opened the door. "Can I come in?," he gasped. She stood looking at him, obviously undecided. "Please, I know who is here. Don't trust them."

He grasped her hand, and instantly, some of his discomfort eased. He knew it would. "Please, tell me what is going on? That is my child you carry. Don't you care at all?"

"Tempest, step away from him." Angelo loomed behind her, and placed a hand on her shoulder. Reaching around her, he removed Michael's hand from hers.

Angelo gently shoved her behind him, and faced Michael. His face was cold.

Michael held onto the door frame, wracked with pain again.

Angelo smiled, one completely absent of warmth or understanding. "You presume too much, Michael. The child might, be yours. Worse, you are not thinking clearly. Do you mean to interfere with us? What we are doing here, does not concern you. Did we request your presence? Have you forgotten your place?"

Michael had never been so afraid. Angelo's anger was barely concealed.

Chao and Sigmud now stood behind him, and Tempest had been effectively removed from his sight! Coming here, facing them, had been a bad decision. He hoped it wasn't a fatal one. Angelo moved to raise his hand, and with lightning speed, Chao prevented him from doing so. He gasped, "Michael, are you ready to leave?"

Michael knew instantly. Chao had saved his life. Angelo was breathing heavier.

His eyes darkened as he glared at him. "Forgive me," Michael whispered, before turning and hurrying down the stairs. Behind him, he heard the door close.

When he reached his car, Michael vomited, more miserable than he'd ever been in his life! And more afraid! That had been too close. He stared in death's eyes, and survived. Survived by a thread. Getting in his car, he waited, trying to settle down. Eventually, his breathing grew even, and the

pain subsided. He didn't know what The Three were up to. Reading them was an impossibility, so strong was their defense. Should he call the Monsignor? If they found out, his life would surely be over. Just for interfering!

Michael lay on the steering wheel, the reality of things washing over him like a cold wave. He had no control. His plans had all gone to hell. Tempest was free of his influence. As always, Paul had won.

CHAPTER THIRTY THREE

The five Monsignors sat around the ornate marble table, steaming cups of coffee before them. They stared at the intercom in the center of the table, listening intently. Monsignor Sebastian verified what they already knew. The woman was the one. The child was coming. Clementine told them of her total infertility. That her pregnancy was now verified. He also told them of Michael's difficulties, and Paul's involvement. He would definitly try to prevent them any access to the woman, no doubt there. But most disturbing, Clementine told them of The Three being awol. None of them knew what to make of that. One of the men, obviously the eldest, with his solid white hair,and crinkled face, spoke first. "Father Sebastian. It's time you return to Rome. We must make solid plans, and prepare for anything Paul may put into action. He is adept at discrediting us, and that is putting it mildly." Clementine agreed, and the connection was broken as he hung up.

All five men leaned back in their chairs and looked at each other. They knew it wasn't going to be easy, but also knew their place in the order. They must acquire the child, and teach it the church's ways. It's power was undetermined, but they must control it!

Monsignor's Thorpe, Randall, Guissepe', Montero, and Arjunto, along with Monsignor Sebastian, and the late Ashe, were the ones assigned to bring this to fulfillment. Find the one of the prophecy, attain the Child of Chance, and keep it safe with the church. There would be no interception for the Fallen. They deserved their punishment, it was ordained. They musn't be allowed to obtain and corrupt the child. They drank coffee, and simply thought about all to come. The main threat was The Three.

As long as they remained loyal, all would be well, but...if they turned on them?

Tempest watched her life be compartmentalized. What did she absolutely need? No, she couldn't call her job and quit. No contact with anyone. Travel light. Suitcases were packed and set by the door. She felt numb. Holding a few of her mother's favorite books, she simply watched Paul
prepare for their flight. That's what it was. They were running. Tonight, a limo would come for them, and The Three would be waiting at a private airstrip, to usher them onto a plane with no flight plan. From there, they would go to Arizona. New names, new lives. She was void of tears. It felt as if she was an actress in a movie, and the script had to be followed, whether it made sense or not. There was a scream within her, struggling like a dying bird, it's wings clipped. If she let it out, she knew windows would shatter, and eardrums explode. This couldn't be happening! Why couldn't she wake up from this dream?

Paul sat the last piece of luggage by the door. He knew Tempest was struggling to hold onto her sanity. But he couldn't help her. He had prayed, and consulted, and the answer was clear. Trust The Three. Protect her at all costs.

Tempest looked at Paul, and some of the panic inside of her subsided.

As long as he was with her, everything would be alright. She could live anywhere, be anyone, as long as he was with her. She smiled shakily, and got up to take her vitamins. Doctors orders. They called it the Child of Chance.

She called it, my baby. Her soft child would be in her arms, for her to love.

To nurture, and kiss, and just love. When Paul suddenly stood behind her, and wrapped his arms around her waist so she could lean against him, she prayed the baby was his. He was a perfect father.

"It will all be okay, sweetie,"he whispered against her hair, kissing the top of her head.

"I know, Paul."

At two a.m., the limo arrived. It was her last friday morning in the house her parents had shared with her. Memories flooded her mind, of them hugging her, or the two of them dancing in the living room to oldies, while she grinned. Sweet, poignant memories. Then she told them good bye, before following Paul out to the limo. In a way, she was as dead as they were. The old, naive, Tempest was no more.

Their suitcases and boxes were packed into the trunk, and she was off to a wiser life. She lay her head in Paul's lap and fell asleep, as they left the city she loved.

Michael woke early, alone and depressed. There was a time when he woke and knew all was well with the world, but those days were gone. All wasn't right with his world. Some of his old teacher's words returned to haunt him. "Your pride and arrogance will only ruin what you could be." Tabor Ashe had said that to him the day before he was killed. And he had laughed at the one man who had probably loved him. Laughed, knowing his days were done. He needed to get up and find something to fill his day. The sun streamed through the window, illuminating the room. He walked to the window to look outside at a perfect morning, and then he knew. She was gone. Tempest was gone. He knew it, as surely as he knew there was an emptiness in him now, that nothing could fill. At that moment of clarity, Michael realized that he really loved her.

Loved her deeper than he'd ever loved anyone. Part of him felt like it was dying! "Don't leave me Tempest. Come back..."

CHAPTER THIRTY FOUR

They drove up the circular drive, lined with cactus which stood taller than a man. They seemed to welcome them with outstretched arms. Tempest couldn't pull her eyes away from the beauty beyond the windows. Sunset on the desert was so surreal. Far in the distance, stood red hued mountains. The desolate terrain was beautiful in its' shadows. So, this was Arizona.

Finally, after the long drive, the house loomed into view, a sentinel on the edge of the desert. It was beautiful! Stucco, with a red clay roof, it blended into the terrain. Simple in design, long and classic. It was surrounded by a covered tile veranda, which offered privacy, and shade. There were no signs of any other homes. They were totally secluded.

Sigmud touched her shoulder, drawing her attention away from the view.

"All of your needs are taken care of. There are caretakers who will shop for you, and provide any of your other needs. But, it is imperative that you follow the rules. No contact with anyone you have left behind. The necessary things, like your job, have already been taken care of. So no one will be worried about you. Just stay here, it is now home. Relax, and enjoy yourself."

"What about finding a doctor, and my health?"

Sigmud lightly touched her cheek. She was surprised by the tenderness in his eyes. "Your doctor, and mid-wife will make weekly visits. They are on call 24 hours a day. All the info is included in the package of papers we gave you."

She shook her head, amazed. "You thought of everything."

They came to a stop. Paul got out and opened the door for her.

Leaving the cool confines of the car, to stand in front of the patio was an experience. The heat was oppressive! The air was full of fragrances she didn't know, but she liked it. Paul kissed her, and taking her arm said, "Let's check out the inside of this place."

Chao and Angelo waited for them on the shaded patio, and ushered them inside. Tempest stepped in, and was dumbstruck. What beauty! It was huge!

Arched doorways allowed one room to flow into another. The Decor was native American, and she adored it. The ceiling lights dazzled with colors of red, sage green, browns and yellows. All of the floors were covered with large, corresponding tiles. Because of the open floor plan, you could see the whole house at a glance. The back walls were glass, allowing an endless view of the desert, and a kidney shaped pool sparkled with the bluest water.

Angelo, always to the point, stated,"No one can sneak up on you with the glass walls we installed. You can see out, but no one can see in."

Tempest touched a low table which held a large flat screen television. She had only dreamed of owning one so big. "This is beautiful," she whispered. "I love this house."

The Three smiled knowingly. "We will go now, and let you settle in. If anyone approaches you, who is not on the list, let us know immediately." Chao glanced at Paul. "You understand?"

"Yes, of course."

They left without saying anything else.

Tempest began to explore her surroundings. Kicking off her shoes, she walked across the cool tiles, and realized the entire house was pleasantly cool. She found the kitchen, and it was fully stocked, of course. How did they know her favorite foods? They were all there. Salmon, Tuna, apples. All the fixings for spaghetti. And so much more.

Beneath the center island sparkled brand new stainless steel pots and pans. She wanted to laugh, like a child at Christmas.

Paul located the bedroom, and just stood there. It was entirely black.

A king size four poster bed sat at the center of the room, covered with black and purple pillows and sheets.The glass wall extended to the bedroom, and the desert at night was breathtaking. Small crystal globes dangled from the center of the ceiling, giving off soft light. Adjoining the room was a bathroom with double sink, and jacuzzi tub. Perfect.

Tempest found Paul staring out the glass at the desert. He was so still, she hesitated to disturb him. He felt her presence, and turned to smile at her, looking more relaxed than he had in a while.

"Paul, this house is incredible. I still can't believe that this is happening. But I feel safer now." She peeked into the bathroom, and spying the tub, stated, "I feel like a bath,...you?" Giving him a blatant come hither look, she ducked into the bathroom, giggling when he ran in and grabbed her.

Michael parked in front of Tempest's house. The protections were no longer in place. He could sense nothing just the same. They were gone.All he could feel was emptiness. It was vacant. Although he knew it was useless, he went in and searched the house. The door wasn't even locked. It was so neat inside, things in their proper places. Dishes in the china cabinet, books stacked in the bookcases. He went into the bedroom, and sighed as he found the bed rumpled. But again, nothing out of place. Michael picked up one of the floral pillows from the bed, and pressed it to his face. He could smell her shampoo. "Tempest,...where have you gone?"

Sitting on the bed, he fought back tears. He couldn't remember ever hurting so bad! She could be anywhere. The world was a huge place, and it had effectively swallowed her up. With Paul protecting her, he didn't have a chance of discerning her. The Monsignor must have lost faith in him, and sent The Three to take care of the job.

He called Clementine on his cell phone. It rang and rang. Finally his acolyte picked up. "Hello Michael," he greeted. "The Monsignor has been called to Rome. I will leave word for him to call you."

So, he was gone to Rome, to meet with the others. No doubt, to prepare for The Three bringing Tempest to them. Filled with impotent anger, Michael shouted toward the ceiling. It echoed inhumanly.

Tempest relaxed against Paul, lazily flexing her toes in the bubbling water. He massaged shampoo through her hair, following the suds that slid across her chest with his hands. She caught his hand, kissed it. Then let him go so he could cup water and rinse her hair.

"Paul, I'm sorry you had to leave everything behind."

"Are you kidding me? Being with you is worth anything." He slid lower in the water beneath her, to kiss the back of her neck.

Cupping her breasts, he smoothly slid inside of her. Tempest gasped, sensation overcoming her. He moved within her, igniting all of her sensitive spots, setting her on fire. Paul grasped her hips, controlling her movements, sliding her up and down in the water, until she screamed her pleasure.

He turned her to face him, and settled her onto him again. "Do I seem sorry to you?," he gasped, slamming deep within her, continuing the motion until Tempest shivered, and tightened around him, holding him close. Only then did he allow his own release, filling her completely. They held each other, gasping, water bubbling all around them.

Tempest gazed up into his eyes, now darker than she'd ever seen them. The pupils were large enough to drown in. She ran her finger down the center of his nose, to his perfect lips. "I love you."

Paul mouthed,"I love you, too" before moving inside her again,gently.

CHAPTER THIRTY FIVE

So many wires. The ultrasound machine was assembled quickly, with silent efficiency. Once everything was operational, the workers left without a word.

Doctor Alain and the mid-wife, Sarah Jackson, smiled satisfactorily. Tempest just grinned, amazed at the way an empty room had been made into a medical marvel.

The Doctor and mid-wife had arrived early, with machines, workers, and boxes of supplies and medicines. None of the workers spoke to anyone but the doctor. They were quick and thorough.

Amazingly, there was no need for her to go to the hospital, or the pharmacy. Everything was there, within reach. A small fridge even held bags of blood, her type.

Doctor Alain helped her onto the GYN table, placed her feet in the stirrups, and satisfied, nodded to the mid-wife. Sarah Jackson was a kind looking woman. She kept staring at her with an expression of wonder. Tempest felt a bit uneasy under her scrutiny.

"I need to examine you. Undress, and I'll be right back. We must speak with Paul for a minute."

Doctor and mid-wife left her alone to remove her clothing and put on a cotton gown, left on the table.

The efficiency of The Three was frightening. How could they possibly take care of so many details, and have the means to hire doctors and mid wives?

Were these people afraid of them, or was it respect? Maybe they were all angelkind, and just anxious for a chance of redemption? She felt like she carried a burden too heavy to sustain. It frightened her. Such expectations, from such a small being. A little child who the Creator was supposed to love so much! Her child. As so often happened, Tempest was filled with doubt. It all was so unreal, yet here she was. In her own private hospital room.

Doctor Alain pulled a letter out, and handed it to Paul, explaining, "Sigmud wanted you to read this, and give your answer."

Paul read the letter, and then crumpled it. He wasn't sure how to reply.

Sigmud wanted to know if he wanted Tempest to have DNA testing on the baby in utero, to discover if he was the father, or Michael. He rolled the possibility around in his mind. Did it really matter? In actuality, he figured the father was whoever it was intended to be. Nothing would change if he knew. In his heart, the child was his because he loved its mother."

"Please tell him it doesn't matter. No test."

The doctor nodded, but added,"Are you absolutely sure? The risk to the mother is minimal, as well as to the child."

"I'm absolutely sure. And no risk to either of them is acceptable."

There were no more questions. They turned and left, to tend to Tempest.

After her examination, Tempest was given an ultrasound. Paul stood holding her hand, watching the image of new life. It was overwhelming, seeing the tiny heart beat. Tempest finally understood it was real. She was carrying a very special baby, one who had defied the odds. A miracle. Tears fell un-hindered. Paul squeezed her hand, sharing her wonder. The mid-wife clicked a button, and the image printed out. Handing it to Tempest, she turned the machine off, and wiped the cool gel from her stomach. "You can dress now. Everything is progressing wonderfully."

Monsignor Sebastian shakily sat down. He pressed the phone tighter to his ear, and mumbled,"She's gone?"

Michael was disgusted, hearing the fake shock in the man's voice.

"Yes, gone. I called you immediately, this morning!"

"How is that possible?" A thin sweat appeared on Clementine's forehead. Horrified, he wiped it away. "Are you absolutely sure?"

"Yes. There's no sign of them. I searched the house, and nothing there to help. Why this performance Monsignor? I know you have arranged for The Three to take care of things, and bring her to you. I wish you could have told me it was being taken out of my hands!"

Clementine jerked forward, his heart racing. Fear infused him. "Did you say The Three?"

"Yes, they were with her. They ran me off!"

"What!!" The Monsignor's heart dropped. The absolute worse scenario was now in place.

"Michael, they have not reported to us at all. They are missing. We don't know what their agenda is! Why didn't you inform us they were in contact with her!?"

"It's understood they are untouchable. You informed us that they are given total freedom. You called them your top men. The Three are your most trusted and well trained,..remember?"

Angrily, Clementine slammed the phone down. He didn't have time for Michael's sarcasm. The Three had Tempest in their control! Finding her was pretty much out of the question, since their resources were endless. In all the years they'd served the Church, they had never made a mistake! Those men were secretive to a fault, and undeniably powerful. What had possessed him to tell them of Tempest? Weren't they Angelkind, regardless of all their training and coldness, wouldn't they want a chance at redemption? He closed his eyes, and bowed his head, but no prayer came to mind. What could he tell the others that wouldn't make it all seem so hopeless?

The Monsignors erupted into outraged conversation at the same time.
"Exactly why did you involve The Three?"
"Don't we have a record of their whereabouts. Where do they live?"
"Have you tried to contact them, to reign them in?"
"This is a disaster. One caused by stupidity."
"We are men of God. Don't lower yourself to name call!"
Monsignor Clementine Sebastian sat, head lowered and eyes closed. He remembered Father Tabor Ashe. Words he'd spoken so long ago. "We aren't the good guys in this." Was God, in his ultimate wisdom, agreeing? Or was this a test of their faith?
The complaints of the others glanced off his psyche, like echoes of a passing storm. They would calm down soon enough. Then what? Even

now the airports were being checked, as well as the trains and buses. They wouldn't find any sign of them. He knew that already.

Hospitals were being contacted, any new patients examined. Clementine shook his head. Another waste of time. They might as well look for a speck of sand in a sandstorm. Tempest was gone. All the years of careful planning, of murder and threats, of secrecy, all of it for nothing! Maybe they weren't the good guys after all.

Michael sat in the middle of his living room. The doors were locked, and all the lights in the house were off. He sat in total darkness. In his hands was a copy of Tabor Ashe's books. All day, he had searched his soul, trying to pinpoint how he'd messed up so badly. Hearing the obvious fear in the Monsignor's voice had brought things to crystal clarity. They all had messed up! He tried desperately to sense Tempest, stretching his spirit in all directions. When that failed, he tried to sense the child. But nothing. Not even a mental wall. She was out of his reach. "It's out of my hands," he sighed, beaten. "Whatever happens, it's out of my hands." A new emotion washed over him. Humility.

CHAPTER THIRTY SIX

Sunset in the desert is spectacular. Pale beige and sun-bleached white

transformed, becoming deep magenta's, warm oranges, and gold.
Beautiful.

Tempest floated in the pool, like she did every evening. She rested on an
inflatable lounge, her hands dangling in the warm water. This was her
favorite time of the day, when everything was tranquil and serene.
Sunset.

Paul stood nearby, cleaning the grill and storing the remnants of
dinner. He watched her thoughtfully, then followed her gaze, toward the
desert. Like her, he never tired of it. But tonight, something felt different
about the approaching night. "Temp! I think it's about time we went in."

Tempest picked up on his unease immediatly. She rolled into the
water and swam over to the submerged steps.

Paul grinned,thinking she was so graceful, despite her swollen
stomach. The five months spent here, alone with her, were precious. He
helped her out of the pool, then stared at the desert again. Yeah,
something wasn't right, he just couldn't pinpoint what it was.

Tempest began to feel it too. A slight change in the environment. A
sense of being watched. She allowed Paul to rush her inside. They
closed the heavy glass doors, and stood staring into the growing
darkness. At least no one could see them, now that they were inside. But
they could see the whole area. Nothing out of the ordinary was visible,
but it was there. No mistaking the feeling. She looked up at Paul and
paused. He stood still, with his eyes closed, intense. "Maybe we should

call for The Three," she whispered.

He opened his eyes and took a deep breath. "I already have."

Michael erupted from his trance, drenched in sweat. His breathing uneven, he looked at the two women sitting across from him. They looked alarmed. He wiped the sweat from his brow, and stood up. "You have to go."

One of the women grew indignant. "We paid for a full reading. You are supposed to be the best, aren't you?"

He glared at her, and she grabbed at her throat, eyes wide. The other woman demanded their money back. "We are only visiting from Arizona, as you know, and can't reschedule."

Tossing the money on the table, Michael snorted, "Take it and get out."

The two women snatched the money up and stormed out, but Michael had already mentally dismissed them.

It had to be by some kind of divine intervention, but he knew where she was! Excitement infused him. He wasn't sure how it'd happened, but he knew.

During the women's reading, an image seemed to form and overlay their mundane life in Arizona, drawing his attention away. He saw a gorgeous home on the edge of the desert, and then,..there she was. The image was pale and soft, like a layer of fine gauze upon the moving images of the women's lives. And then it was gone. But just that glimpse was enough. Somehow, her energy must have infused the energy of Arizona itself. He knew where Tempest was!

He packed quickly, thinking of calling the Monsignor, and firmly dismissing it. He no longer had any plan. Michael simply wanted to see her, to be with her in any capacity, to know the child. Probably his child, but actually, the child of all of them, the Angelkind.

Chao entered the house first, looking calm, despite the urgency of their summons. He walked over to Tempest, and lovingly touched her stomach. She felt the baby move, and slowly, her heart calmed. Looking at Paul, he nodded. "We felt it too. A disturbance."

Sigmud and Angelo came in. "It's clear now."
Paul stared outside, and relaxed. Whatever had been there before, was gone. Everything felt normal.

"It's Michael, isn't it?" Tempest suddenly knew. "He's found us."
Chao nodded. "We do believe you have been detected. Very likely by Michael. He retains a bond, you see."

Angrily, Paul sucked his teeth. "A bond. Any bond has been broken."

Chao didn't react to Paul's anger. He looked at Tempest, and nodded. "There is a bond,..if the child is his."

She looked into his eyes, soft, and barely human, drowning in the dark irises. "He'll come after us, won't he?" Tears filling her eyes, she turned away. She was bombarded by the hurt emotions Paul was feeling. This was horrible.

Angelo took control. "If Michael comes, we will take care of him." Tempest clenched her hands at those words. "You'll take care of him how?"

"That is up to you." Angelo smiled slightly, and it was frightening.

Paul heard the terror in her voice, and intervened. "You can't kill him. Tempest couldn't deal with that."

"Why?" Angelo looked from Tempest to Paul, his face a blank. "It would effectively remedy the situation."

For a space of time, everyone was silent, as if waiting. Tempest looked at Paul, loving him even more for understanding. Then she faced The Three, and admitted, "I don't think he's done anything horrible enough to be killed for."

Angelo crossed his arms, and blandly challenged,"Well, do you wish to give him the chance to do something horrible enough,..to die for?"

Sigmud interrupted, and changing the subject, suggested they wait and see.

There would be surveillance on the ways in and out of the state. They would know Michael's every move. And if they were mistaken, and it wasn't him after all, they would still be on alert. He went to Tempest and gently turned her toward the bedrooms. "This has been stressful for you. Go and rest. It's good for you and the baby."

She managed a smile. "You just want me out the way, so you can speak with Paul."

"That too."

She walked to the bedroom, having no desire to hear their conversation.

What did Michael want with her now? Was he going to try to give her to the Church? After all this time?

Chao stepped outside with Paul, and together, they simply enjoyed the night. It was coolest at night, and almost pleasant. Paul knew that Chao was the most diplomatic of The Three, so this conversation wouldn't be agreeable.

He waited.

"Paul. You are extremely possessive of Tempest."

He sighed. "No, Chao. I'm devoted to her."

"You were never one to play with words. You understand what I'm saying. You must also understand that she cannot belong to only you. She and the child must belong to something larger. It may one day be a necessity for you to separate."

Paul stiffened. "Never gonna happen."

Chao touched his shoulder. "Don't be foolish. None of this is in our hands."

"I know. What do you see?" Paul felt as if something was clawing at his heart. He asked, but he really didn't want to know!

Chao knelt and picked up a stone. He turned it in his palm thoughtfully.

"I don't see anything concerning you and Tempest. But I sense something, like the first inkling of a storm. It concerns you, Tempest,..and Michael. You hide from something that you already know, and that is your right. But,..it can affect your lives. We want to discard of Michael, but you prevent it. If things get beyond your control, if Tempest is in danger, we will kill him. Despite both your wishes, and hers."

Paul shook his head in denial, but Chao merely turned and went inside.

Tempest hugged the pillow and closed her eyes. She didn't want to move again. This home was comfortable and she was beginning to feel the discomfort of her pregnancy. How on earth had Michael found her?

Had he alerted the Church already? It still hurt that he wanted to place her in their hands. She wished she'd been strong enough to avoid him altogether. But her ego and inexperience had landed her right in his clutches.

Tears squeezed out of her eyes, and she buried her face in the pillow. Deep inside, she knew who her baby's father was. She felt it. And even now, the baby moved restlessly within her. What was she going to do?

The last thing she wanted to do was cause Paul any pain. She loved him so much! She was full of questions that she didn't dare to ask. When her baby was born, what would happen then? Did the Angelkind expect her to give her child to them? She could never do that! Would they have them in some kind of seclusion, waiting for whatever was supposed to happen, to happen? How would they know if The Creator suddenly decided they could be redeemed of the sins of their ancestors? Would the Fallen Ones suddenly be freed of the punishments handed down to them?

So many questions! Her life was one huge ball of uncertainty! And the most frightening question of all,..what if nothing happened?!

A soft knock sounded at the door. Sitting up, she wiped her tears away.

"Come in."

Paul entered. "They're gone. Are you okay?"

Tempest shook her head yes, not trusting her voice to be steady. She didn't want him worrying.

"You know everything will be okay, right?" Paul sat next to her, and reached over to wipe remaining wetness from her cheeks. "No need to cry."

She grabbed his hand. "I'm ,Paul. I'm scared on so many levels."

He wasn't sure how to respond. Maybe the truth was best. "I'm afraid too, Temp. Afraid that I'll lose you somehow. Or that all of this will be for nothing."

Surprised, Tempest looked over at him, relieved that she wasn't alone in her doubts. "What if things get violent, Paul? If Michael and the others try to take me by force?"

Paul grinned, stunning her. "Oh Tempest, hon, you don't know The Three."

"There are only the three of them, no matter how powerful and connected."

Laughing softly, Paul warned, "Don't confuse them with some kind of Mafia or gang. The Three are much, much more than all that. They were trained from the age of 13 in all the martial arts. All the ways to kill. Stealth. Their Angelic skills are extremely advanced. There are three of them, yes. But they operate as one. One mind, one body, one objective. Few of us have actually met them. They were almost a myth."

Tempest couldn't believe anyone or anything could be so totally powerful. She thought about all she'd just been told, and couldn't grasp all of it.

"Who trained them?"

Paul shrugged. "The story is that three young men, around the ages of 17, approached a priest after an Easter mass, in Rome. They knew about the circle of Monsignors who handle our kind. And they wanted to be,..handled."

He chuckled. "Supposedly, they were already extremely well trained. They soon climbed to such a place of esteem, that they are merely known as The Three. And they are deemed untouchable. I wouldn't worry too much, if I were you."

"So,..why would they turn against the church now?"

Paul nodded in agreement, but added, "Why did they really show up in Rome in the first place?"

CHAPTER THIRTY SEVEN

Michael looked out across the airplane's wing, to see the sun bathed clouds outside his window. All of the beauty was wasted on him however. He had other things to think about. It wasn't going to be easy. Once he found Tempest, he had to get past Paul, and The Three. That wasn't going to be easy. Then he had to earn her trust somehow. No, this wasn't going to be easy by any stretch of the imagination. He was relieved that she wasn't in the Church's clutches, as he'd feared. So what had The Three been talking to her about at her house, those many months ago? If they were involved even now, then his chances were almost nil. But,..worrying didn't help. So much of this was out of all their hands. He stared out the window and sighed, "Tempest, you made me love you. Don't throw me away."

Angelo sat in the limo outside of the airport, glaring at Chao and Sigmud.

"What is wrong with you two?," he snapped. "Let's grab him as soon as he gets off the plane! We can dispose of him in the desert, and no one needs to know he was ever here!"

"Will you listen for once!" Sigmud shook his head, frustrated.

"Yes, listen." Chao leaned forward in his seat, and spoke softly, forcing the other two to lean toward him, just to hear. "Don't you think it strange that he was able to locate Tempest? I am almost certain he fathered the Child of Chance. That cannot be ignored. I have thought about this, and perhaps his part is not played out. Michael may be important in some way, to the Child's survival, or even his purpose. What if, by destroying him, we destroy ourselves?"

Disgusted, Angelo sighed, "We all know what Michael is. He has always been the dark to Paul's light. He is dangerous."

"And we are not?" Sigmud grinned at him. "What are we? How much blood is on our hands? And you are still anxious to shed more. The time is near, where we can be judged as man is, and forgiven. But how much do you expect to be forgiven for? The fact is that the three of us may never be forgiven."

Angelo fell silent, fear on his face. He looked to Chao, but the other man held his head in his hands. Disturbed, Angelo looked at the airport exits, not knowing what to say. Sigmud touched his shoulder in understanding. "When he steps through those doors, we will kindly escort him to the car, and take him with us. He will have a chance to declare what his plans are, and we shall take it from there."

Angelo nodded. For once, he was speechless.

Michael stood among the throng of people passing in and out of the airport. There was relative safety in a crowd, but...

He saw that the taxi's waiting in front were rapidly being grabbed up, so he stepped to the curb at a quick pace, before they were all gone. An arm linked with his on both sides. On his right stood Angelo, his left, Sigmud. "Will you make a scene?" Sigmud asked, his face emotionless. Michael sighed, and replied, "Would it do me any good?"

"No."

Resigned, he let them lead him to a black limo with dark windows. It gleamed obscenely in the intense Arizona sunlight. The heat hit Michael like a blast when he left the airport. Now he was a prisoner it seemed. "Wherever you are taking me, please say there will be A/C." To his surprise, Sigmud laughed.

The limo was very comfortable. The soft, black leather seat adjusted to him perfectly. Chao handed him a glass of chilled wine. So civil, Michael mused, as he fearlessly took a sip. One of his many questions was now answered. The Three were still involved with Tempest. "Do you plan to hurt her?" he asked, taking another sip of the exquisite wine.

"Never," Chao firmly stated, his eyes seeming to bore into his soul. Michael squirmed under his scrutiny. "Then what do you want with her?"

Smiling coldly, his teeth feral, Chao asked,"Do you have the right to ask any questions, after the demise of,..Tabor Ashe?"

Michael caught his breath, and set the glass down very carefully. "I had nothing to do..."

"Michael, michael." Chao shook a finger at him like a patronizing older brother. "We know exactly what you did. He was the one person who loved you, your mentor, and yet, you set him up for execution. We suspect it was all over jealousy, of Paul."

Michael was actually surprised by the swell of guilt and regret that filled him upon hearing those words. He didn't want to remember!

Chao leaned forward in his seat, across from him, and firmly placed his hand upon Michael's chest. It was like an electric shock! Images filled his mind with violent color.

The sun! That April morning the sun had been so bright, and warm. A beautiful day. Tabor Ashe wasn't feeling that well, and slept in late. Michael had argued with him the night before, just like he always did. He argued about not being taught enough. He argued about not being told enough secrets. And of course, he argued about favoritism for Paul. Maybe he was the reason Tabor hadn't felt good, because he felt such anger for the man!

On this beautiful day, he decided that he had no more need for Tabor. He called Monsignor Clementine and told him where they were. He also told him much more. That they were close to locating the woman who would bear the Child of Chance. And that Tabor had hundreds of documents that should be given to the Church.

Plans quickly fell into place, while his mentor slept. Find a reason to go to the neighborhood park, and they would take it from there. They would bring Tabor in, and bring him back to the fold. Michael would be rewarded with recognition for his skills, and inclusion to their plans.

Tabor was easily led to that park. He liked it, and found it to be a peaceful meditation spot. Michael didn't even have to argue with him. He was looking forward to just being free of Tabor after today. He was sick of having his feelings hurt, and being disappointed. He'd rather be back with the Church, where they knew how special he was.

They sat on a familiar bench under a very large, old pine tree. Tabor opened his worn satchel and began to go over a stack of papers, marking it with a pencil ocassionally. A dark blue sedan pulled up, blocking the park gate. Immediately, Tabor became aware of it, and stuffed his papers back in the satchel. "We need to get out of here," he whispered to

Michael, patting his arm. Instead of getting up, Michael gripped Tabors arm tightly, preventing him from moving. At that moment, understanding dawned on the older man, and his eyes filled with tears.

"My Michael. This is what I always feared. But I am not sorry to share the fate of our beloved Joshua."

Angered by those words, Michael squeezed Tabors arm painfully. "You aren't Jesus, old man. And I'm not Judas!"

Four men walked over from the sedan, and dragged the struggling Tabor out of the park. Michael began to follow, but one of the men gave him a warning look. "You,..go home. A car will come for you in the morning."

As the car pulled away he caught a glimpse of Tabor, looking out at him. His eyes were full of pity.

Chao pulled his hand away, and Michael jerked back through time, to the present. Tears stung the back of his eyes. He looked at Chao, feeling like he'd been stabbed.

"Only now do you really feel what you did? How odd." Chao noticed the tears in Michael's eyes. "Even I will not force you to relive the following day. The day Father Tabor Ashe was found dismembered. Murdered. Now, we will ask the questions. What are your plans for Tempest?"

Michael looked out the window as they drove past strange scenery.

He felt purged. Weary. "I just want to love her. I want to love my child. I want to help them in any way I can. I just want to be forgiven." His words surprised him just as much as it surprised The Three. But they felt the truth in them.

Angelo shook his head. "Idiot. I hope you're aware that you led the Monsignors right to her. I know they have a watch on you. To them, once a traitor, always a traitor. They don't trust you."

Michael sat up straight and snapped, "and you don't either. So be it. But I need to see her!"

Angelo, Chao, and Sigmud simultaneously relaxed into their seats and closed their eyes. Michael wondered if they were shutting down somehow, or communicating. Probably communicating. He was very aware that his life hung in the balance. But Tempest was so close. He knew it!

The limo smoothly raced along the busy road. The Three remained totally quiet, and Michael began to feel as if he was alone. It was strange to be surrounded by these men, yet they felt non-existent. An hour passed, and the empty silence remained. "I'm dead," Michael thought, staring out the window. "They are going to kill me now."

After a half hour, all three opened their eyes, and stared at him. Battling a growing fear, Michael stared back, his gaze steady.

A hint of a grin appeared on Chao's face. "Michael. We will take you to her. Paul is there as well. We will see,.."

Tempest prepared a large dinner. All day, she'd lay on the couch and slept. She felt exhausted. But now, she was ravenous. She knew Paul was puzzled by her behavior, but there was no explanation for it. It simply was how she felt. Tempest diced a red and a green pepper, before throwing them into a bowl with onions and mushrooms. Adding a healthy dose of garlic, she put the mixture into a pan with melted butter, and began to sautee all of it.

When she checked the chicken breasts roasting in the oven, she wished she could tell Paul of the whisper that began in her head that morning. Michael was coming. He was coming soon. Even more disturbing, her child was moving a lot within her, as if excited!

The wild rice was done. "Keep busy," she told herself. Laying the chicken on a bed of rice, she poured the sauteed mixture over it. The smell was heavenly. There would be company for dinner. A strange sort of reunion.

The limo pulled up at the house at her favorite time of day. Sunset. She was placing food out on the table. Paul looked at her as he had all day, confused, wary.

"You don't seem surprised that there's company," he mused.

She just smiled, placing the main course in the center of the table, within easy reach of all the chairs.

Paul sighed deeply, and as the doorbell rang, he whispered, "It's Michael,..isn't it?"

She looked up at him, the answer in her eyes.

"Damn! You could have warned me."

He opened the door to find The Three standing there, as well as Michael.

Shocked that they'd bring him here, Paul hesitated to invite them in. Chao raised an eyebrow, waiting. Deciding to trust them, Paul stood aside so they could come in. Chao touched his arm. "We will be civilized." It was more than a suggestion.

Tempest stepped out of the dining area to wave them in. "I imagine you all are hungry. Come have some dinner." She looked from Paul to Michael, hiding her nervousness.

Michael's breath caught as he saw her. Still beautiful. Graceful. And her stomach,..she was showing. He wanted to grab her close and claim her, and hurt anyone who got in his way. Then he felt Chao's hand on his shoulder, returning him to sanity. He would be the one to get hurt.

Angelo looked at Sigmud and shook his head. He mumbled, "Civilized, alright." Sigmud chuckled and nodded.

They all walked to the dining room and sat down. Paul was quick to sit next to Tempest, so Michael sat across from her. He was afraid to speak. All he could do was stare at her. She hadn't changed much. The Arizona sun left her with a rich, becoming tan, and a bit of pregnancy weight, that was all.

Angelo, Sigmud and Chao recited prayer, then began to fill their plates, talking among themselves animatedly, as if unaware of the other three tensely feeling each other out.

Paul's eyes bored into Michael's. Why couldn't he just give up on her? It was time to just give up! Michael looked back at him with a cocky expression.

"Okay Paul, I get it. I'm a bother. But I won't give up. You wish I'd just disappear. Not gonna happen."

"What do you want from us?" Paul leaned forward in his seat, anger spilling from him.

"I want you to understand that Tempest is carrying my child. So I, too, want to protect her. I even love her."

"You don't know what the hell love is!"

"At one time, I didn't. But, when I lost her..," Michael smiled at Tempest, and it was atypically soft,"I realized how much I love her. How much I need to be near her, near them."

Tempest reached down beside her,and clasped Paul's hand in hers. He calmed some.

"It doesn't matter if the baby is yours or not, Michael. You forced her to your will, to your bed. How much of it was her free choice? Only you can be truthful about that, Michael. How much was really her choice, and how much was skillfully manipulated by you?"

Michael thoughtfully played with his rice, swirling his fork through it.
He looked at Tempest and admitted. "Not much was of her free will. I mesmerized her. But despite all of that, some of our time was real. I taught her to trust her skills. And together, we made the Child of Chance. There has to be a reason for it."

Tempest waited for Paul to argue about the parentage of her baby, but he didn't. It seemed he felt it was Michael's. The baby kicked strong inside of her. She looked over at Sigmud and asked, "Isn't there a paternity test I can take, very soon, to prove who the father is?"

"NO!" Both Michael and Paul protested at the same time.

Angelo laughed, and it was strange indeed, coming from him. It was more an amused sort of bark.

"Well Sigmud? I can call the doctor and find out. That will take care of part of the argument."

Paul argued, "There is a test, but there's a risk of miscarriage. It's not worth the risk."

Michael nodded firmly. "I agree."

Tempest leaned back in her chair to rub her stomach. Maybe her little one would settle down some. "Michael, what were your plans, when you first came after me. Did you plan to give my child to the church? What?" She watched the emotions play over his face. He's open to me, she realized.

"I realized who you were when I came to your office to feel you out. I was supposed to locate the woman most likely to bear The Child of Chance. You were one of several located years ago, and actions were put into motion by the Church to isolate and keep track of all of you. It soon became apparent that you fit all the signs, and your blood was verified. After that day in your office, I decided to change those plans. I would seduce you, bond you to me, and possibly father the child with you. I pretended, but never planned to give you to the Monsignors." Michael took a deep breath. "I planned to keep you and the child hidden with me, and become most important of my kind. They'd look up to me when my child freed them. And I'd have you."

Paul was horrified. "Damn, Michael! You were always selfish, but this surprises even me!"

"Oh right, Paul, the perfect one. The one who got such special treatment from the elders, who stole Tabor's affection from me. I was the special one, until you came with your big, sad eyes. I was your friend! But you left me anyways! You always left me, off to do big things."

"You fool! I left because I refused to be part of all this. I wouldn't kill for them! I refused to interfere with the higher plans for this child!"

"You did interfere!" Michael stood up, his silverware clattering. "She was mine, and you interfered! What were your plans all along, but to have her for yourself. Are we so different after all?"

"The very sin that got our kind into so much trouble." Sigmud's voice silenced everyone. Michael sat down, wearily. "Yes Michael, Paul. That was the greatest sin. To interfere with Yahweh's new creation. To hunger for the human women, and bear children with them. That sin still has so much power over us. Look at the two of you, once like brothers. Now filled with hatred."

Tempest took a bite of her food, and chewed slowly, mulling over Sigmud's words. She looked at The Three, seated so righteously. Then she looked at Paul and Michael, seemingly broken. "No one at this table is perfect," she stated softly. "Sigmud, Chao,..Angelo, haven't you killed for the Church? Paul, Michael, the Church used you as well. I'm far from perfect. So, I figure we have to either trust each other, and find a way to exist together, or this Child inside of me doesn't stand a chance." She began to eat in earnest, as if unaware of the five men staring at her in wonder.

CHAPTER THIRTY EIGHT

The murmurs from the other room were oddly comforting. Tempest
felt safe. Really safe. She put the dishes in the dishwasher, and was
thankful that dinner had gone so well. She could breathe again. For a
while, she thought Paul and Michael were going to come to blows.
Thank goodness everyone had calmed down. Michael was a quandary.
He felt different from the man she knew.
The man capable of such cruelty, and who tried to murder Paul. He felt
broken somehow. Waves of nausea didn't fill her, and she was able to
feel his emotions now. He had let his guard down. She wanted to make
peace with him, but she didn't love him. Not like she loved Paul,
passionately. Paul was her peace, and her storm. His arms were perfect
shelters. She could remain entwined with him forever. Tempest took a
deep breath. Then why did she feel that Michael needed to be with
them? It didn't make sense!

There was a sudden change in the atmosphere, just as Paul raced into
the kitchen. Snatching her around the waist, he led her to the rear
archway, leading into the hallway to the bedrooms. The sound of
breaking glass resounded around them. There were shouts, and more
breaking glass. Paul led her out through the bedroom to the pool area.

Tempest was so afraid, she didn't want to breathe. Any sound could
give them away. Someone screamed as if in agony. A vehicle, like a
small jeep, backed up over the beautiful patio, cracking the tile, and

stopped near the pool. The door opened and she could see it was Michael. More pained and agonizing screams filled the air. Lightning flashed overhead, as if to give light to the scene below. Michael beckoned to them to hurry and get in. A man appeared in front of the jeep, dressed all in black. Michael shifted gears, and rammed into him, sending him rolling over the hood to lay still on the ground. "C'mon!" he shouted at them.

Paul ran with her and shoved her into the car first. His eyes locked with Michael's.

"Get in!" Tempest cried, seeing something in that look. Something she couldn't describe. "Please Paul!"

Paul opened the rear door, then froze, his stance awkward and off balance, like a puppet. A short distance behind him a man like the one Michael hit, stood, a gun smoking in his hand. "Go!,"Paul gasped, before collapsing.

Michael hit the gas, squealing over stone and sand, racing past cactus and hills, into the dark and silent desert.

Tempest saw something in the light from the house, as they sped away.

Chao appeared behind the assassin and with ease, snapped his neck. She began to scream for Paul, but he didn't appear, it was still. "Michael, go back! Don't leave him!!! Go back!!!" She hit him, tried to grab the steering wheel, but Michael was wooden, his eyes on the terrain. He wouldn't go back, she already knew that. To them, all that mattered was the child. Hot tears filled her eyes, and she balled up in the seat to cry for her love, her Paul. She didn't care anymore.

Chao got in the limo, as screams filled his senses. Angelo and Sigmud could take care of the rest, he had to locate Tempest and Michael. He looked at Paul laying unconscious in the back seat. He had done the best he could, but he needed a doctors care. They had miscalculated the speed of attack. They had made a mistake, the first! How had they been so careless?

He pulled out to the road, rolling over black clad bodies, and maneuvering around several jeeps and cars. Desperate, the Church had used a full frontal attack, and they should have forseen this! Chao was so angry. He sped away, headed for Doctor Alain's office. He would drop Paul off there, and then try to locate Michael. He hoped that Tempest was safe with him.

Angelo stabbed two fingers into the base of the man's throat, gagging him.

When the man caught his breath, after much retching, he asked, again, "What are the plans?"

The man was young. He stared through wet blue eyes. "Plans?"

Angelo dug two fingers into his left eye, and dug it out. Holding the mass in his palm, he waited for the man to stop screaming. The other two men tied up near Sigmud, screamed too.

Sigmud looked at them coldly. "None of you are going to live through this night. It will be an easier death, if you talk."

Angelo leaned over to wiggle the bloody mass in his palm near the man's remaining eye. "See this?" he asked. "This is what happens when you ask stupid questions. We know the Circle of Monsignors sent you. We know that Michael led you to us. Did he do that knowingly?"

"No, no, he had no idea!"

"Just let us go!" one of the others shouted. Sigmud kicked him in the stomach to silence him.

"What are the plans?," Angelo asked again, very softly.

The man dropped his head, blood dripping on his chest. "We were to kill everyone but the woman. We were supposed to bring her to the airport and transport her to Rome."

Angelo leaned closer. "And if things went wrong,..what then?"

"We must kill her and the kid."

Angelo wrapped his hands around his throat. "You will not feel this," he murmured close, as he squeezed tighter and tighter. The man sat motionless, a calm look on his mangled face. Then his remaining eye rolled up, and he was gone. Angelo looked closer, then let go of his neck.

The other two men began to kick frantically at their bonds, begging and shouting. Sigmud placed his hand on one of their chest, held it and willed the heart to stop. Soon the man was dead.

Angelo did the same to the other.

They walked outside and turned to face the house. They looked at the bodies scattered outside, then together, they made the decision. Holding thier arms up, palms toward the house, they stated, "Burn."

Flames licked up from the foundation, and quickly engulfed the house.

They dragged the bodies close to the inferno, watching as they ignited. Then they got into the closest car, and drove away to meet up with Chao.

Tempest woke to total darkness. She struggled to scream, but someone held her close, and covered her mouth. She remembered everything. Paul's stricken face, the way he fell,..all fight left her body. The hand was removed.

"You should have gone back," she moaned.

"He would of never forgiven me." Michael whispered. "You know that."

"I don't care!" Tempest moved away from him, trying to adjust to the dark. "Where are we?"

"Hidden. We are in a crevice. I sent the jeep off by jamming a stick and a rock on the gas, and carried you to this crevice. We're hidden well."

She closed her eyes, and the image of Paul's face filled her vision. She should have died with him, holding him. The tears fell, as she thought of him.

"Tempest, we are a strong breed. Remember how he healed from the accident?"

"How can you bring that up!?" Tempest wanted to kill Michael. He deserved it, not Paul!

"I'm just saying, don't assume he's dead. The Three will see to him."

A tiny flame of hope ignited. "Do you really think so? What if they were captured, or killed?"

Michael snorted. "From what I could see, The Three were inflicting serious damage. I never saw men move so fast!"

He fell silent for a while, and she was thankful. Tempest wanted to pull herself together, try to come up with a plan.

"Tempest,..may I?"

"What, Michael?"

"May I touch your stomach?"

There was a hint of a little boy in his voice. She wondered what had turned him so dark. What had really happened to the little boy he'd once been?

"Alright."

Michael reached out and touched her abdomen, and the child kicked against his hand. A strong kick. He caught his breath, and felt something fill his heart so intense, he wanted to cry. Tears filled his eyes. He was thankful
Tempest couldn't see it in the darkness. But he knew at last what real love was. He would die for this child. Leap from the tallest cliff if he had to, for this child. Reluctantly, he removed his hand and pressed it to his chest.

Tempest felt the baby kick inside of her, upon Michael's touch. Any remaining doubts disappeared. She carried his child. Somehow, through his awful designs, Michael had fathered a miracle. She turned away from him as much as she could in the small space, filled with mixed emotions.

Dr. Alain entered the reception area, where Chao sat impatiently. He looked tired, but relieved. "Chao, you can go and find them. Paul will heal.
He needs to rest. The bullet didn't hit any major organs, but it's a nasty injury just the same. Just missed his spine."

Chao nodded. "We care for Paul."

The doctor nodded his understanding, before returning to the back office.

Sigmud and Angelo entered quietly, unsure what to expect. Chao stood and smiled, to relieve their minds. "He will be alright." They visibly relaxed.

The Three stared at each other for a moment, then Chao nodded. "So, the monsignors decided her death would be acceptable." The other two nodded.

Angelo added,"And Tempest is now right where Michael wants her, in his posession."

Chao sighed. "The question is, what will he do with his,..advantage."

They left the office in a hurry, afraid to find out the answer to that question. All three piled into the limo and sped away, searching the darkened road along the desert for any sign of them. It was time to call in help. A full search was necessary.

Tempest dozed off. She was terribly uncomfortable in the small confines, and thirsty. And she wanted more than anything to find out any news about Paul.

Her mind simply needed rest.

Michael carefully wrapped an arm around her shoulders and leaned her toward him, so she could rest more comfortably. We're in a shitload of trouble, he thought, listening to her breathe. For all he knew, there were assassins searching the entire desert for them right now. He didn't feel any sort of threatening presence, but that didn't mean it wasn't there. Tempest was pregnant, and couldn't really be expected to traipse through the brush.

They needed water and food. Damn. Where were Chao and the others?

He thought about Paul. The way he'd stared at him, just before being shot. He knew what was about to happen, and trusted him to care for Tempest.

Michael looked down at her, resting on his shoulder. Paul trusted him to care for her, to save her. Damn. Right now there was only one thing he could do. He hadn't done it in some time, but it was time to travel. Closing his eyes, he meditated. He meditated until the sounds of the desert, of Tempests soft breathing, all faded away. He concentrated on only one thing. Chao's face.

Chao's rational face. He felt the sudden separation of body and soul, and he was above, looking down at his body, still next to Tempest. This freedom felt so good! Immediately, he found himself in the limo, staring at the Three. Focusing on Chao, he stated his wherabouts, then quickly, was drawn back to his body. Re-entry was uncomfortable, and breathing heavily, he allowed himself to fall asleep. They would come for them now.

Feeling Michael's presence, and hearing his words, Chao relaxed in the seat, relieved. He knew Michael could be trusted now, and Tempest was alright. He made a quick call on his cellphone, and turned the car around. They would all meet at the airport, and there were plans to be made. It was time to move.

Sigmud mumbled sleepily, "She will want Paul,..immediately."

Chao made another call, and replied, "An ambulance will transport him to the airport. She will see him,..immediately."

With a smirk, Angelo went to sleep.

CHAPTER THIRTY NINE

Monsignor Sebastian sat at the table, his mind in a jumble. What in the world had gone wrong? They had the element of surprise. The men were their best, and not one survivor! Tempest and her protectors were in the wind again, and this time, Michael was with them! What a disaster.

"Clementine?"

Monsignor Arjunto was staring at him rather coldly.

"Yes?"

"Am I correct to assume that The Three have no problem killing their blood brothers? The very assassins who trained at their side? Is that a correct assumption?"

Clementine focused on his hands, pressed flat upon the highly polished table. "I would have to agree."

Arjunto got up and walked to an ornate chest, to extract a bottle of aged wine. "Will you join me?"

"Glad to."

For a length of time, the only sounds were the ticking of the grandfather clock near the entrance, and the clink of glasses as they drank the wine. Monsignor Clementine broke the silence. "We must come up with a plan."

"Hmmn, a plan. What would you suggest?" Monsignor Arjunto sounded sarcastic, which grated on Clementine's nerves.

"When are the others due?"

Arjunto snapped, "When they get here. Don't you realize how serious this is!? We've lost her!! And worse, she is protected by our elite!! The Three are experts since childhood. Michael is volatile, but talented. And Paul!! Such talent which if tapped into, would rival The Three! So, what kind of plan can we possibly devise?"

Clementine balled his fists, and fought to control his temper. Arjunto was prone to panic, so this was no exception. But to speak to him in this way!

Taking a steadying breath, he snapped, "I suggest you pull yourself together. They might think you've lost your faith! We must believe we will find them again, and this time, we won't make any mistakes!" When Arjunto appeared to calm down, he continued, "We will pray through this night for guidance and help. For deliverance of The Child of Chance into our righteous hands. We will not lose faith. His will be done."

Michael stood in the tower, and looked out across the entire island. The view was incredible! The full moon shining down on the silver waters, reflecting a million stars. Greece was as beautiful as she was ancient.

Chao had suggested he have a look, and he was glad he did. It was magic. It also took his mind off the fact that Tempest slept in Paul's arms. There was the gentlest of breezes. It was fragrant with all the flora of this isle, and it soothed his heart. For a moment today, Paul was like his friend again. The only friend he'd ever had. But how could he accept being second best? How could he simply forgive him for all the anger and pain he'd caused him? Or,..was he the one in the wrong? "Am I my own worst enemy?"

The grecian night, full of peace and splendor, lulled Michael into his own soul searching. Some of the answers he discovered surprised him.

Tempest lay folded in Paul's strong arms. She snuggled closer, loving his scent. The soft lull of his breathing. It was a night of memories. Where was the insecure woman who had waltzed into Maggie's shop, and taken a chance?

That woman who used arrogance to hide her insecurity, what had happened to her? Tempest couldn't recognize her old self anymore. She was afraid now, but also very happy. She knew her purpose. She was in love. And miracle of miracles, she would be a mother. It felt like she was encased in a bubble of warmth, and affection too great to name. Paul sighed in his sleep, and tightened his hold on her. Yes, she felt surrounded by love, sacred and human.

She felt complete. Closing her eyes, she let sleep take her.

Michael woke to the sound of the loud whirring of helicopter blades. He was disoriented, but soon realized he fell asleep in the tower. Looking out, he recognized the approaching chopper as the one that brought them to the isle. He stretched his cramped muscles and wiped his face with his shirt.

Then he rode the lift down, to see who was coming.

The wonderful aroma of eggs, and steak filled the air. Tempest and Paul sat at the table eating, so he relaxed. They weren't in any danger. Two women entered the room, accompanied by The Three. Their eyes searched, and focused on Tempest. Smiles lit their faces as they approached her. Michael tensed. Who were these women?

The younger woman extended her hand to Tempest and introduced herself. "I'm Doctor Apollia. And this is your mid-wife, Alexandra. Are you ready for your exam?"

Tempest wiped her hands on a napkin, and stood to accompany them upstairs. Doctor Apollia took her hand. "Has there been any more pain?"

"No. I feel good actually."

The woman nodded. "So glad to hear that. I still need to do an internal exam. Also, to check your vitals."

Tempest smiled, liking the woman's energy. "I'm a good patient. We can go upstairs to my bedroom."

Alexandra spoke, her voice like a childs. "We are following this pregnancy blindly, in a manner of speaking. We can't be sure it will be normal in all ways, for it is a special pregnancy. So please, any discomfort, tell us immediately."

Those words filled Tempest with alarm. "What do you mean? Something could go wrong?"

"No, no," Alexandra soothed her by patting her shoulder. "I'm just saying that we have to pay close attention. Some with angelic blood tend to come early, and be very vigorous in the womb. And this little one is special. So we want to monitor you closely, and make sure all is ready when the time comes."

Dr. Appollia rubbed Tempest's hand. "Don't worry. Alexandra is a very thorough person. She did not intend to worry you. Everything is fine."

Everything had to be fine. Tempest pushed all negative thoughts aside. Of course things would go well. It was foolish to worry. But, what if something did go wrong? How could they handle it here? It wasn't equipped, like in Arizona. She looked at Paul, but he seemed calm, and gave her an encouraging grin. Yes, of course she was being foolish. It was hormones. All pregnant women worried. She led the doctor and midwife upstairs, so she could be examined. Please, she prayed, let everything be normal.

Paul watched them climb the stairs, his heart racing. Why hadn't he ever thought about something going wrong with the pregnancy. To say it was a stressful one was an understatement! And the mid-wife had opened her big mouth, panicking Tempest. He saw it in her face, her body language.

He walked over to speak to Chao, but Michael got there first.

"Listen, Chao,..Tempest needs round the clock care," he blurted, "What if something goes wrong?"

Paul sighed loudly. "Shut up, Michael. Please?"

"I have a right to speak. It's my child, after all. Not yours!"

Paul reached toward him, but managed to control his anger. "Lower your voice before she hears you. Do you want to upset her?"

Michael stepped away from him. What had he felt..just now. When Paul reached toward him? His chest hurt so badly! "What did you just do to me?"

Confused, Paul snapped, "What are you talking about?"

"He isn't aware of what almost happened," Chao chuckled. "Shut up Michael. It's safer that way."

Paul looked at him, not understanding. What did he do? Michael stared at him with something close to fear on his face.

"What did I do? What's going on?"

The Three began to chuckle, and something about that terrified him. Paul faced Chao, trying to understand what was so funny. "I won't like this thing you find so funny,..will I?"

He was acutely aware that Michael had backed away some distance from him, still looking humbled. All he'd done was reach out to attack Michael, but he'd restrained himself. What was so shocking about that?

Chao stopped smiling and stepped up to Paul, placing a hand on his shoulder. "Don't be upset. What happened was natural for you. You were told you were special, weren't you?"

"Please Chao. Don't start that."

"Why did you run Paul? Why do you fight what you are? We expected you to come to Rome and train with us, ..and then you ran away."

Paul could hear all the old plans being laid out for him, in that other life..in the church. He could feel their expectation, and disappointment.

"I'm not a killer. I refuse to do it."

Angelo folded his arms and lay his head to the side, studying him. "You would kill for Tempest."

"And only for her. Her, and her child."

Chao squeezed his shoulder slightly, and stated, "You just hurt Michael."

Paul wanted them to just shut up! He didn't want to have this conversation, and he wanted Michael to stop looking at him with fear! "I never touched him!"

"You did touch him. Your mental power touched him. Your very thoughts touched him, and caused severe pain." Chao released him. "You felt that force leave your body,..didn't you Paul?"

"I know how to control myself. And no, I didn't feel a thing."

Chao chuckled. He glanced at Sigmud and Angelo, knowingly. "There is this fact Paul. We are who we are. We are born with certain gifts, and that cannot be changed. Eventually,..we all find our way to our own truth. And then, we can truly become."

Paul felt overwhelmed and under attack. Why did they insist he face this, now? His mind was made up. A killer he wasn't. "I'm not good with riddles," he stated, firmly. "And I'm done with this conversation. Michael looks like he'll live."

Stiffly, he walked away from them all to join Tempest upstairs, and make sure she was alright. He hated the way The Three had laughed about all this.

As if they understood what he was going through, and were amused by it. It had been so easy to just work in the shop, and take life easy, until the right woman made her presence known. But now..with Michael on his case at every opportunity, it was hard! He had to maintain control!

Tempest dressed, and asked any questions she could think of. "Is she gaining weight?"

Doctor Appollia chuckled. "You think it's a girl then?"

Tempest had to laugh. "I guess I do. Is it okay if the baby moves alot? She moves alot at certain times,..like when Michael is near. Hard kicks."

The doctor smiled warmly. "Okay, your baby is a bit large for six months, but that isn't unusual. Everything is fine. Your vitals are excellent, which is a blessing, given all you've been through. The more your baby moves, the better. Near the end, they get rather tight in there, and slow down considerably, just resting for the big push."

Alexandra laughed softly. "We'll give you the blood results in a few days. But everything looks wonderful."

The next question was embarrassing, but it bothered her, so Tempest asked,"Is it okay to still have sex, this far along?"

Alexandra blurted out a large laugh, then covered her mouth. "Honey," she teased, "that is fine all the way through. But no acrobatics please. I believe that having healthy sex leads to an easier delivery."

"I'm glad to hear that!" Paul entered the room, a huge smile on his face.

The doctor and midwife were obviously embarrassed, but Tempest simply laughed. "Better safe than sorry. As usual, your timing is impeccable."

"I try sweetie, I try."

Paul sat on the bed, a smile plastered on his face. He winked at Tempest and she laughed again. "You are ridiculous. Stop grinning like a cat watching it's cream."

"Nice description. So correct."

Tempest and Paul grinned at each other, as if no one else was present.

The doctor and mid wife promptly excused themselves, going downstairs.

"Good thing they took off. I thought I would have to take you right in front of them. I want you really bad right now." Paul removed his shirt, his eyes never leaving hers.

Tempest grew warm inside. She doubted she'd ever tire of looking at his well defined muscles, and smooth skin. When he unzipped his pants, she stepped back a step, and teased, "You want me right now? Even with this huge stomach of mine?"

"Everything about you is perfect. Every round curve, and taut muscle. Just perfect."

Paul awoke a sensuality within her that erased any feeling of being awkward. His hot eyes consumed her from across the room. Tempest unbuttoned the front of her dress, and let it slide to the floor.

Holding his arms out to her, Paul huskily commanded, "Come here."

She walked over to him, oblivious to the fact that so many were downstairs, probably aware of what was happening. She could care less. She stood in the circle of his arms, and sighed as Paul kissed her stomach, lay his cheek against it, whispered something she couldn't understand. She bent over him, kissing the soft curls on his head, holding him close. He slid his hands upward, cupping each of her breasts, kneading them, evoking a moan from her as heat spread through her body. Her legs weakened and he pulled her onto his lap as he continued to worship her body. Touching her, gently gliding his hands across her skin to find each curve, to knead and caress each part of her. He slid a hand between her legs, and finding her wet, slid a finger inside of her.

Tempest trembled, softly screamed. His touch was like an electric current coursing through her veins. Leaning back against him, she enjoyed the sensation of him exploring her within, as he had done without. Carefully, he lay back and rolled her onto the bed. She lay spooned against him, his arms now encircling her.

Paul slid into her slowly from behind, holding her comfortably against his hard body. Pressing against him, she wrapped an arm around his neck. They moved together, like an incoming tide, cresting the beach until the tide fully rode in, exploding on the shore. He covered her mouth as she screamed her joy, kissing her neck, her back. Paul stilled, deep inside of her, and waited for her breathing to calm. "I love being like this," he sighed, moving again.

Breathless, Tempest whispered, "I love it too. Just being close to you like this, away from everyone." She pressed back against him, until he filled her. Paul moaned loudly, and she was deeply satisfied. Tempest took control, giving as he gave, until he shuddered against her, holding her tight, giving all of himself to her.

They lay together, simply enjoying each other, listening to each others synchronized breathing.

"Paul,..I love you so much." Tempest reached back to hold his arm.

Paul looked at the curve of her neck, and love overwhelmed him.

"Baby. I'd kill for you."

As The Three led Doctor Appollia and Alexandra out to the jeep to drive to the helicopter, Michael paced the floor. The pain in his chest had subsided, but not the fear. When had Paul become so powerful, and how had he hidden it all these years! After trying to kill him, he was lucky to be alive!

For all this time, he'd been playing with fire. Only Paul's honed control, and innate fairness, had kept him alive. He was sure of it now. "If he had actually touched me, I'd be dead now," Michael mused aloud, his heart racing.

But he simply could not understand why Paul fought against, and concealed such power. Why hadn't he, like The Three, anihilated the attackers in Arizona. This changed things altogether.

Michael looked up at the ceiling, imagining what was happening up there.

His chance of regaining Tempest's heart and bed had pretty much slipped away. Paul wouldn't allow that. Besides, she had made it clear that she loved him. Damn! The only thing in his favor, was that the child was his. And he knew it was, with every fiber of his being. He had fathered the Child of Chance. And there was nothing Paul could do about that, no matter how powerful he was!

The Three watched the helicopter lift into the air, the powerful machine turning and heading towards Skiathos, soon a mere dot in the distance. Sigmud lifted his head, letting the sea breeze waft over him. "Brothers," he said softly, "Paul completes us."

Chao and Angelo nodded, almost solemnly. They watched the wispy clouds drift across an azure sky, their eyes bright.

Sigmud continued, "It is difficult to simply stand by, and watch things unfold. To wait for him to come into his own. But we also know it is the only way to claim him."

Angelo blurted, "Michael is a difficult part of the equation. He is difficult to endure."

Nodding his understanding, Chao added, "But he is part of the equation none the less. He is here for a reason. We can only guess what it is, but there are no accidents. No coincidences."

Angelo sighed heavily, then turned toward the jeep. "We must go back and keep an eye. It is as dangerous within the house, as it is outside."

They got in the vehicle and headed back up the path.

Night descended on the isle as slow and gently as a prowling cat. With it came a comfortable silence. Tempest lay on the couch watching the news. The usual array of gunshot victims, war, and politics. It all seemed so far away.

Beautiful, large candles flickered in the corners, bathing the area in a comforting ambiance. She peeked around and saw that Paul was in the surveillance area with Chao and Angelo. Sigmud was in the kitchen area with Michael, preparing dinner.

She got up and walked outside to stand on the porch and absorb the isle.

There was a pleasant, fragrant breeze. It was still hard to believe she was in greece. A place steeped in myth. Stories of Gods, and half Gods, of lessons hard learned. How fitting it was, to be here, now.

Michael came out with a chair for her, then went back inside, saying nothing. Tempest was grateful for the silence. The baby moved slowly inside her womb, then was still again. "Be patient," she whispered, sitting down.

The sky was so huge here, and so clear. She could almost count the stars.

Each glowing sparkle was closer than the planets beyond them. And beyond the planets, galaxy's. What lay at the end of all those galaxy's? The Creator?

Or did he really hold all of this vast creation in his hand, too huge to comprehend? She held her stomach protectively. Something so vast, so all powerful and encompassing, would love her child enough to change his mind?

It didn't seem possible. What was this child, but a dot in creation. Yet the Creator of all that, would notice that dot, and love it? Tempest wondered how she could be blessed with such a miracle. Because so long ago, her ancestor Mary was blessed in much the same way? She was surprised when the tears fell, sliding down her face as gentle as the night. The moment felt sacred, because for the first time, she really dared to believe. All doubt was gone.

Paul came out with a chair, and sat next to her. "Enjoying the night?"

"Oh yes. Just having a little prayer session, in my own way." She gave him a brilliant smile. "Thank you for finding me, and guiding me. For loving me. It's the only way I could have ever accepted all this."

Paul simply leaned over to kiss her deeply.

CHAPTER FORTY

Skiathos' religious community was abuzz. The Archdiocese had sent out alerts far and wide, inquiring if anything seemed amiss in their communities. Were there any new comings and goings, or strangers arriving? Well, this island was used to coming and goings. It entertained many visitors throughout the year, tourists anxious to sample it's history. One thing came to the mind of Father Temple and Anachos. The helicopter traffic out to the secluded and uninhabited islet of Tsougkria. They had often discussed the lack of tourists booking to enjoy its quiet beaches. Just the helicopter. God-awful loud thing that it was.

Would Rome find that interesting? Could he actually be promoted for being alert and involved with his parish? Father Anachos crossed their church, and peered out the window, in the direction of the islet. "I wonder what is going on," he mused. "Seldom does Rome involve itself with small matters. This seems to be something huge, for them to send feelers out like this."

Father Temple agreed. "It won't hurt to send a notice to Rome about our suspicions. Won't hurt at all."

The two priests set out to prepare a letter stating that the only thing they found out of the ordinary was the lack of travel to Tsougkria, and the military helicoptor that seemed to fly there occassionaly. It was probably nothing.

Tempest lay in bed, uncomfortable, and wishing everyone would leave her alone. She was in mild labor. For two days, irregular pains wracked her spine and abdomen. Doctor Apollia and the mid-wife, Alexandra, had set up house there, not wanting to leave her side.

She was almost eight months along, and so tired. Michael paced the room with a tight expression. Paul lay in bed with her, talking to her soothingly, trying to make her comfortable. "Where are The Three?," she gasped, as another pain coursed lazily across her lower spine. A mere tease of what would soon come.

Paul brushed her hair from her face with a finger. "Sigmud is in the tower, keeping a watch. He feels uneasy today. Chao is on the front porch, and Angelo is downstairs."

Tempest looked at Michael. "Please," she begged, "Stop pacing. It's driving me crazy."

He sat in a chair against the wall, pouting.

She turned away from him, aggravated. It had been close to impossible to endure him these past weeks. All Michael did was stare at her, or try to beat Paul in making her comfortable. Every once in a while, he tried to plead his case, using his fatherhood of her baby. Right after it was born, she intended to demand a test, and although she didn't have much hope, she prayed it was Paul's. The next pain to hit her was considerably stronger, and she moaned softly. Paul placed his hand flat against her lower back, and she could feel heat seep into her bones. It felt good.

The doctor and mid-wife were preparing what would be needed.

Towels, the epidermal, and even bags of blood in case of emergency. An entire section of the bedroom had been transformed into a medical facility of sorts, sterile and handy. It made her feel more secure. "She's almost here," Tempest whispered to Paul, her excitement growing. He smiled his brightest. "Yes, and you'll hold her in your arms."

Sigmud stared toward the beach and shook his head.. No, not now! A helicopter was approaching, and it wasn't theirs! Closing his eyes, he sent word to the others.

Below, Angelo raced up the stairs and burst into Tempests room. He took in the situation, but there was no help for it. "Paul, Michael, move her below to a safe room. We have visitors!"

The doctor nudged Alexandra into action, folding what they needed in clean towels, to transport.

Tempest cried out, "we're under attack?!" A crushing pain spread through her abdomen, and her water broke, soaking the bed. "I can't move," she sobbed, looking at Paul pleadingly. Saying nothing, he jumped to his feet, and reaching down, lifted her in his arms. "Hold tight," he ordered, striding to the stairs.

Michael grabbed the two hospital poles and followed. Apollia and Alexandra followed him. They all reached the main floor and could hear the sound of helicopters. Angelo pressed the wall, revealing one of the spacious bathrooms. He had already put towels and blankets in the tub, as well as pillows. "Sorry Tempest," he said softly, ushering them in. When Paul placed her in the tub, the door slid closed behind them.

Tempest tried to breath, but it felt as if her windpipe was closing. She kept thinking of the Arizona attack. The deaths. Her baby! She held onto Paul's arm, her eyes wide.

"Calm down." He placed a hand on each side of her face. "I'm here. Michael is here. We won't let anyone hurt you or the baby. Breathe."

Chao took a deep breath, closed his eyes, knowing instantly that Sigmud and Angelo did the same, and began to speak, reinforcing the protections erected around the property. Many would die this day, and one was coming, one worth more than all of them.

Angelo shut off all the lights, blew out the candles, in preparation. The intruders weren't familiar with the place, they were. It was a major advantage. He finally stood by the door, and waited.

Sigmud returned to the tower. The helicopter had landed on the beach. It would take time to find them. That was good. He counted ten men. A mere ten, the fools. But then he noticed another helicopter on the horizon. Night was fast approaching, which was good for them. Darkness was always best for battle. He smiled crookedly. Paul might find himself this day. That would be best of all. He rode down to join the others, excitement coiled within him like a whip. It had been inevitable they'd be found. Their forgiveness would not be so easily given. So be it!

Tempest curled on her side as Dr. Apollia inserted the intravenous, miserable as pains came closer together, with regularity. Terrified, she listened to the pregnant silence. Why now? How had the church found them?

Paul didn't like the silence. What was going on outside the door? He couldn't sit here and expect The Three to protect all of them, alone. But Tempest clearly didn't want him to leave her. Her eyes followed him wherever he moved. Michael watched them, as always. He wore a thoughtful expression. Paul frowned under his intense scrutiny.

Tempest cried out with a pain, and both men looked at her, alarmed. The mid-wife held her hand, and draped a cool cloth on her forehead.

Michael told him, "You know you should be out there, defending her. Deep inside, you know that."

Tempest reached for Paul, giving Michael a warning look, but he continued, "I would go, but I am not as strong as you, Paul. It is not my place. I will guard this door with my life,..but you will prevent them from ever reaching this door. I understand now."

"Paul, stay with me. Don't listen to him! He just wants you to go so he can see my baby born. I need you to be with me, not him!" Tempest pleaded with all she had, before another pain took her breath away. The doctor looked at both men. "This baby is coming very soon."

A sound filtered through to them. Gunfire. Paul knelt beside the tub to hold her close. He kissed her, trying to ignore her tears. "I have to go help them, Temp. They shouldn't do it all alone. I will be back. I will." He untangled herself from her grasping hands, and walked to the exit.

Michael reached out and touched his arm. "I wish I was you."

Paul looked at him coldly. Darkness was creeping into his soul, and it felt awful. "Careful what you wish for." He touched the wall, and as the door slid open, he gave into the dark part of himself. No one would hurt her while he was alive! As the door slid closed behind him, he headed outside where he instinctively knew The Three waited.

Paul stepped onto the porch to find the house surrounded by men. They were standing a distance of several feet, and some shot at the house, but nothing happened. Sigmud and Angelo stood on the porch, seemingly relaxed, and somewhat amused. Sigmud looked at him, and asked,"How is she doing?"

"It's really close. Anytime now."

"Well, glad to see you. Those fools will get through our barriers eventually." Angelo knelt down on one knee, and touched the wooden porch, whispering. Sigmud added thoughtfully, "Some of them are angelkind. Not extremely gifted, but clever. The rest are human. They will figure out how to remove our energy field, and then,..they will die."

Paul started to deny that, but then he thought of what they would do to Tempest. And they would take the child away and lock it up and train it like a slave, hidden from all of them. Never! He growled, "Yes, they will die."

Angelo smiled.

Chao was in the rear yard, holding up his protections as best he could, but it was weakening. He could feel the vibrations of the invisible shield beginning to thin. It was to be expected. But within he felt joyful. Paul had come out to help. Of his own accord, he'd decided to really fight. From the corner of his eyes, he saw three camouflaged men creeping into position. They pressed to the treeline, sighting guns on the tower. He sighed, "I see you."

They began to shoot toward him, noticing he stood alone, and he grinned as the bullets disintegrated against the shields. Chao outstretched his hands toward one of the men and shouted. The man burst into flame, screaming as he literally began to melt. As the other two ran to his aid, Chao repeated the action, igniting them like matches. They flailed, screaming horribly. Folding his arms, Chao whispered, "And then there were none."

Some of the bullets were getting through. They pierced into the wood of the porch, the wall. The dirt on the pathway. Sigmud snapped, "They're getting through. Game time." He pulled a gun from his side, to Paul's surprise. Angelo
carried a huge, serrated knife. They heard loud screams from the rear of the house. Angelo chuckled. "Chao is alert."

Paul thought of Tempest. She must be so afraid. Was the baby here yet?

"Push Tempest. You can do it. All that matters is the baby." Alexandra leaned forward as Tempest pressed her legs against the side of the tub. The midwife positioned her legs for an easier delivery.

Michael sat in the tub behind her, letting her lean against him in a sitting position. He felt helpless, as she sweat and cried.

Tempest pushed, trying to breathe through the pain that threatened to rip her apart. She wanted Paul!

As soon as the shield failed, five men ran forward, guns raised. Angelo leaped from the porch and ran straight at them. He flung his knife, and it buried itself in the leaders forehead. With a snap of his wrist, the weapon returned to Angelo, and he flung it again, taking another down. It happened quickly, and the men attempted to scatter. Sigmud shot all three in their moment of confusion.

Paul watched this with increasing admiration, unsure of what he should do.

He heard shouted commands, and a trio of men tried to rush the side of the porch on his left, and what happened was without thought. It was instinct.

Paul saw a blackness fill his vision, as if the moon was hidden behind a bank of clouds. There was a burning in his eyes, and he leaned forward, staring at them intensely. All three men crumpled, smoke rising from their bodies. He saw their exposed skin split, and ooze. A rush of adrenalin filled him, and something else. Pleasure. There was the loud sound of shattering glass, one of the windows. Chao's shout could be heard, then more agonized screaming. Paul stood, ashamed and energized at the same time.

He saw Angelo run to a man trying his best to crawl in a window to the right. Quickly, the man was tugged from the house, and Angelo then clawed at his throat, ripping. The man lay still, and Angelo wiped the blood from his hands on his pants. He was smiling widely.

Something was wrong. Michael could feel Chao's distress right away.
Sigmud and Angelo were busy at the moment, ending the lives of other men trying to reach the porch, so he raced to the back, bullets whizzing past him. Even as he ran, he realized that for some reason, the bullets couldn't touch them.

Four men held Chao in the dirt, trying not to get too close, but holding his arms and legs. Paul shouted as it happened again, the veil of darkness, the burning in his eyes. But he didn't want to hurt Chao! Chao shouted, "Do it!"

Paul leaned forward, as if supported by a strong wind, and released the energy painfully filling his mind. The four attackers fell like broken dolls, smoke wafting up in the fragrant night air. Falling to his knees, Paul tried to bring reason back. It was hard. He was anxious to release the power again, to kill again! Chao was at his side, helping him to his feet. "Don't think,"he snapped, "Act. Tempest needs us!"

The air felt electric, and each person approaching seemed to glow in the night, ethereal. Together, Paul and Chao reached out to them, and they fell like leaves upon the dirt. Some ignited into brilliant torches. It felt amazing. Paul felt in tune with everything around him, beneath, above, on all sides. The thoughts of The Three flowed through his mind like gentle whispers. Everything had a glow, or spirit, even the bullets he dodged so expertly. Amazing. And beneath it all, he could feel Tempest, closer to death than she'd ever been, but so full of life.

Alexandra looked directly into Tempest's tired, frightened eyes. They had all heard the sounds of the battle taking place outside, but the baby wanted to be born, now. She whispered, "One more push sweetie. One more strong push and you can hold your baby in your arms, okay?"

"I'm so tired. I just can't."

Michael added, "You can do this. When Paul comes back, he'll see you holding your child, and he'll know it was all worth it." Michael's heart felt raw. He didn't tell her how badly he wanted to see his child. Or that he knew it would probably be the only time he'd feel like it's father.

He couldn't challenge Paul, and he couldn't win her love. The most he could do was help her through this torment, and be there for her now.

Tempest heard his words, and pictured Paul coming through the door, and coming to them, showering them with kisses. Holding her child, love in his eyes. Mustering her remaining strength, she pushed hard, ignoring the pain, pushing to her last breath.

Alexandra shouted, "Good. There it is!" She guided the baby from the canal and cradled it in a soft white towel. It was a girl. Doctor Apollia cut and sealed the cord.

Bright blood began to gush from Tempest, flooding across the towels beneath her. Tempest fell back against Michael, limp. Alexandra whispered, "Let her hold her." The doctor placed the child on Tempests chest, and began attempting to stop the bleeding.

Tempest felt so cold. So weak. She hugged her daughter and smiling, examined her fingers, her toes. Wide almond shaped eyes stared at her. Wise eyes. A bag of blood was hooked to her intravenous port, but she only saw her daughter. Her perfect little girl. "You were my purpose," she whispered, kissing her. Michael rocked them against him, tears flowing down his face. They were losing Tempest. He could feel it.

Doctor Apollia removed the afterbirth, felt inside her for a tear, frantically trying to save this special woman. Blood was everywhere. They should of been in the room upstairs, full of light and room to move. Not a tub filled with towels and pillows! Alexandra kept fluids pumping into her, crying openly.

Tempest stared into her baby's round face, finding it hard to breathe. She wanted to look at this face forever. Overwhelming love filled her, and then the little girl nuzzled at her chest. She was barely able to, but Tempest tugged her top down and began to nurse her child. The cold feeling was rapidly spreading through her body. She felt so sad, but not afraid. Part of her would continue to exist, and her daughter was so loved, by so many. Her life had great meaning, and she was blessed to know what it was.

Doctor Apollia was trying her best, trying everything she knew how, but somehow, Tempest knew it was no good. It was time for her to go home. She kissed the top of her daughters head, and collapsed against Michael.

"Don't leave us," he whispered, tears in his voice. "Please Tempest? fight. Stay for Paul. For your daughter."

Her words barely above a sigh, Tempest said," Not up to me. Tell Paul I love him." Tempest closed her eyes, slowly fading into a comforting peace.

"Oh God, no! We're losing her!" Alexandra put another bag of blood up to drain, as the doctor stitched a ragged tear in the uterus.

All four men stood still. Sigmud, Chao, Angelo, and Paul. No one moved on the perimiters, and silence fell. This portion of the battle was over. They all felt the presence of the Child of Chance. It was here. The very atmosphere heralded this souls arrival.

Paul felt the slow ebb of the bloodlust, as normalcy returned to him. He also felt more. Tempest was dying. The feelings of satisfaction and competency that killing had given him, gave way to near panic. She was dying!

He ran, crashed through the front door, reached the wall and pressed, activating the bathroom door. The sight that greeted him stabbed at his heart.

Alexandra crouched near the sink, sobbing. Doctor Apollia sat at the foot of the tub, her head lowered, blood saturating her hands, arms, and gown.

Tempest lay still, the baby on her chest sleeping. She was leaning back against Michael who was wet faced, and red eyed. No. He couldn't wrap his mind around this. She was sleeping. That's what it was, sleeping.

He walked to the tub and whispered,"Tempest, it's me. They're gone." There was no response. He reached down and touched her hand. It was growing cold. "Temp. Say something, babe. I'm here."

Alexandra cried louder. Paul lifted the baby from her chest and cradled her in his arms. He looked at the sleeping child, seeing Tempest in the tiny face. Then he turned to Michael. "You let her die."

Michael whispered, as if sound would disturb her. "The doctor tried to stop the bleeding, but it was too late. I'm not a healer. I couldn't do anything. She wasn't like us, you know that. She couldn't heal herself."

A rage was building inside of Paul. He wanted to destroy everyone who had let her drift away from him. The doctor, the midwife, Michael, the attackers. He wanted to obliterate the very vatican and all within it's walls! Trembling, he held the little girl close, fighting the rage, the tears. He willed the feelings to settle inside, to coil and remain still. Finally he could speak again. "Michael, get out of the tub."

Michael obeyed, careful not to Jostle Tempest as he did so. He gently lay her on the pillows.

"Remove that bloody shirt."

Michael did so quickly, afraid to speak. He could feel the restrained anger coursing through Paul, and he didn't want it directed at him.

Paul gently handed the child to Michael. Michael grasped her close, his heart once so bitter, breaking. "Paul, she was at peace. She told me to tell you she loves you."

Not replying, Paul looked at Doctor Appollia and Alexandra. "Get out. I need to be alone with her." He closed his eyes, the pain of loss overwhelming.

"You too Michael. Get out."

When he heard the door slide shut behind them, Paul approached the tub and sat on the floor. He removed the bloody towels and pillows from beneath Tempest, very carefully. These he shoved against the wall. Then he gently removed her clothing, finally letting the tears flow. Crying silently, he touched her face, the face that had become his sunrise and sunset. "What will I do without you? How could you leave me?"

Running the hot water, he began to bathe her, the last respect and comfort he could ever give the woman who owned his heart. This woman, who could calm him with her touch. Without her, he felt lost. He cried out like a wounded animal, no longer able to contain his pain.

CHAPTER FORTY ONE

Sigmud sat before the blank television. He had no words. Upstairs, the Doctor and midwife were helping Michael to clean and dress the baby. "She has no name," he said without emotion. "I truly liked Tempest. Her child must have a name." Angelo, who paced behind the chair, stated, "A name will come to her." Chao sighed heavily. "Think what Paul must be enduring now. He fought bravely for her, and lost her just the same. Didn't he come into his own today?"

The other two nodded. All three thought this was beyond unfair, but dared not say it. It wouldn't change anything.

Chao looked toward the hidden room. "He's been in there for two hours. How long do we let him mourn?"

Angelo snapped, "We leave him alone! He was lucky enough to find love, and now it's gone. He will have as much time as he needs."

"We understand that. But I am sure another attack will follow. Even now, they furtively retrieve their dead." Chao stood up. "I will miss Tempest. There was a gentleness and giving in her soul. She accepted this burden bravely. But do not forget we have a baby to protect. A baby which is now totally dependant on us. There is no time for lengthy mourning."

With an unseemly grunt, Angelo mused, "I doubt Paul will agree."

Sigmud gasped angrily, "Can you not hear his thoughts? He blames himself! Paul believes that by killing, and joining us, he did wrong, and her death is his punishment! How do we undo that? He can react several ways, one being to deny what he is from now on!"

The bathroom door slid open, and Paul stepped out. He looked drained.

"Chao. I am going to bury her. Right on this island."

Angelo held a hand up. "It isn't exactly safe out there, brother."

Paul lifted his head. "I defy anyone or thing to stop me." His voice was cold.

Sigmud murmured, "your daughter needs a name."

The look Paul gave him was dark and dangerous. Deadly. "That will have to wait. I must bury her first."

Angelo walked up to him. "The sheilds are once again operational. I can assist you."

"Thank you. I need one of her dresses."

With a quick nod, Angelo headed for the stairs.

Michael sat on the bed, holding his daughter close. She was now clean and dressed in a cotton gown, with matching booties. She was staring at him with vivid blue eyes, his eyes. She deserved to be nursed by her mother, not fed with bottles. She must already miss the beat of Tempests heart. Michael had thought himself incapable of tears, yet he cried so much this night. He held a finger by her hand, and she grasped it immediately. Trust. This little one trusted that she'd be taken care of.

The doctor hung up her cell phone, exasperated. "The pilot tells me that he hasn't been allowed to come to the isle. There is a story out that the area is contaminated. He said he'll fly out anyway, without reporting it, and bring formula and bottles, everything a baby needs. If you want to leave this place, that is when you must do it."

Michael kissed his daughters soft head. "The Three will make those kinds of decisions."

Angelo came in. He looked at Michael, then the baby. "Is she doing well."

Michael nodded. "She is wonderful."

Dr. Apollia repeated her story to Angelo, and waited. He didn't give her an answer. "I came up for one of Tempest's dresses. A pretty one."

"What is going on?" Michael was alarmed.

"Paul intends to bury Tempest on this island."

Alexandra selected a nice, simple dress for Tempest. One easy to put on.

Angelo took it and thanked her. "If you hear anything out of the ordinary, don't be alarmed. Stay inside. No danger will come to you."

"Doesn't Paul want to see the baby,..hold her?"

"He will,..in his own time." Angelo left them, dress draped over his arm.

Michael rocked the child in his arms. "Looks like it's me and you, sweetheart. Everything is okay. I can hold you forever if you need it."

Paul carried Tempest carefully. She was awkward in his arms, a shell. But he kissed her lips lightly. She was all he had of her, and soon, even that would be gone. He walked out the door, and Angelo followed.

It was growing light, the sun just beginning to rise. The bodies of dead assailants were gone, as he knew they'd be. Somewhere, they were under observation, but it was quiet. No one dared approach them. He carried her to the back, and studied all of the thick growth at the treeline. Without much effort, he extended the area of protection, and walked confidently into the trees.

Angelo watched him for a moment, a bit surprised. This was an entirely new Paul. He wasn't sure what to expect of him. The essence of Paul's sorrow was hard for him to absorb. He finally followed, keeping at a respectable distance. Paul wanted to do this himself, so he would keep watch.

Paul placed her on the ground in a small opening in the trees. Rays of sunshine were beginning to filter into the spot, illuminating the beautiful flora all around. The spot was perfect. On his knees, he began to dig with his hands, pulling up fistfuls of dirt, remembering everything he and Tempest had shared with each handful.

"Dead!" Monsignor Clementine Sebastian was horrified. He had so hoped to avoid that possibility. "What of the baby?"

The man before him shrugged. "We have no idea. We don't even know how she died, since access to the house was never accomplished. Maybe a stray bullet."

Clementine folded his hands on the desk, so tightly that they became numb. Once more, their plan had failed. There was no surprise attack, since they were sighted from a tower of some kind. And as if things couldn't get worse,..

Paul fought with The Three. Reports claimed the four of them were too powerful to defeat. Their skills seemed to have increased, and Paul had found his power. Good Lord! Tempest was dead, which meant he must be full of anger and fury! Was the child alive, or dead with its' mother? What a mess!!

"Alright,..what is our next move?"

The man hesitated.

"Tell me."

"Most of your umm, angelkinds, have simply walked away. It was very strange. They got quiet, staring at each other. Then,..they simply left, despite our orders not to. My men are not willing to go in without them. We took huge losses in the battle. Those men don't wound,..they kill. And I swear they enjoy it!"

The monsignor dropped his head on his hands. Either the child was born, and they felt it's presence, or dead, and they felt it's loss. There was nothing to be done,..for now. His faith was taking a huge blow, but there was nothing to be done.

"Pull out. Observe the premises from a safe distance, but no action."

"Understood." The man smartly turned, and left the office.

Day came, its heat more subdued than usual, with a strong seabreeze. The helicopter arrived with fresh supplies, but Paul continued to dig, and Angelo watched. The doctor and mid-wife were returned to Skiathos, and still Paul dug. Angelo left just once, to get water for him, and he still watched, as angels of old. The helicopter returned to the clearing down the path. The

pilot entered the house, and all was silent.

When darkness fell, Tempest rested in the earth, lovingly placed there by Paul. He pat the dirt and kneeled upon it, completely worn out.

Angelo approached him, and without a word, helped him to his feet. Slipping an arm around his waist, he supported him on the walk to the house.

Without a word to anyone, Paul entered the bathroom.

Michael sat watching television, holding his daughter, now dressed in a nightshirt. He looked at Angelo questioningly.

"It's done. I'm sure he will shower, and talk to us."

Michael wasn't so sure that he'd ever really talk again. It was disturbing, this silence that Paul surrounded himself with. His thoughts were no longer open. What if he simply faded away from everyone, even the baby?

Such a thing would of broke Tempest's heart! "His silence worries me. What if he never comes out of this?"

Angelo shook his head. "If he doesn't return to normal, we must accept that."

"Accept it?" Horrified, Michael looked down at the baby in his arms. "If he doesn't accept this baby, my baby, as if it was his own,..then Tempest will not rest. She loved him,...till the end, she loved him. She wanted this child to be his. Even though I love my daughter, she is like Paul's daughter too,..even to me."

The Three stared at him, in shock. This didn't sound like Michael. Had he undergone some kind of transformation? Tempest had truly been magic, in that case. Sigmud looked at the child more closely. She looked very much like her mother, but the eyes were undeniably the bright blue of Michael's. He wondered if Michael had been led here for this very reason. So that this little girl would have at least one of her parents with her. "She is a beautiful child. Anyone who sees her will love her, including Paul."

"I hope so." Michael kissed her lightly. "He needs to name her. Maybe he and Tempest had picked out a name." The tiny baby stared up at him wide eyed.

Paul showered. He looked down at his feet, at the muddy water swirling around them, and then turned the heat up, wanting the hot water to hurt, to burn. Maybe it would wake him from this stupor that he felt. She was gone, and it simply wasn't fair! Why was she taken, when her child needed her, and he needed her? Maybe if he hadn't gone out and fought, he could of saved her.

At least he would of been with her at the end, instead of Michael. She had begged him not to leave her! Regret churned in his gut. While he killed assassins, satisfaction filling him with his power, she had bled to death.

No! He had cried enough! It was time to face reality, and that was that she was gone, and he had to protect her baby. His baby, regardless of what Michael felt. He calmed himself and dried off. Time to face the music. Wrapping a large towel around his waist, he looked toward the corner where he'd shoved the bloody ones. They were gone and he was grateful someone had removed them. He didn't want anymore reminders of his loss.

He stepped out and saw everyone around the baby. Michael was feeding her a bottle, and The Three were watching. Even the pilot sat nearby. Walking over to them, he hesitated a moment. A surprising thought assailed him. This little one had killed Tempest. Angry that the thought even filled his mind, he took a deep breath, and looked down at her. Her resemblance to Tempest was uncanny. The same heart shaped face. The tilt of wide almond shaped eyes. She looked up at him, and he saw their brilliant blue hue. Damn. The identical blue of Michael's eyes. He reached down for her, expecting Michael to resist, but there was none. He handed her to him with ease.

Paul cradled her in his arms, drowning in her eyes. She was so beautiful it was ethereal. He touched the soft hair which hugged her head, checked the tiny fingers. She was perfect. For this time, he forgot the others watching. It was just him, and the baby. "Your mom wanted you so badly," he whispered to her, kissing her. "She loved you so much, sweet one." Paul rocked her, walking slowly back and forth across the room. "We all love you." Her eyes never left his, as if recognizing him. "I may not be your daddy,..but I feel like I am."

She blew a milk bubble, and he had to smile, wiping it away. Softly, he began to sing to her. Tempest had loved his singing. The baby did too, for she fell asleep in his arms. He looked over at Michael, who was watching, with a small smile on his face. "What do you think of the name Mariah?"

Michael's smile broadened. "I think it's perfect."

Paul turned to the pilot, and softly, so he wouldn't wake Mariah, he told him, "Go with someone to inspect the copter. We need to gather everything, and get out of here."

Sigmud went outside with him. Michael and chao began to gather clothing, and the baby's supplies. They filled a box with dried goods, and a few weapons. Paul handed the baby to Michael and mumbled, "She needs both of us. Agreed?"

"Understood."

They made their way to the helicopter, unhindered. As they lifted off, Paul stared straight ahead, lost in his thoughts. What now? He wished he had a plan, but somehow,..everything seemed out of their hands.

CHAPTER FORTY TWO

After three flight changes, a visit to a doctor to have the baby's health evaluated, and limo ride, they boarded a private flight which took them to the mountainous state of Montana.

The Three had a large van waiting at the small airport where they touched down. After all the provisions and bags were packed in the trunk, and everyone seated comfortably, they drove through gorgeous scenery. The rich bluish greens below the mountains, and yellows of the cultivated fields, and swaying grass of the flatlands, against the constant backdrop of blue sky. This was big sky country, and it deserved it's name.

By nightfall, they arrived at a cabin close to the Missouri River. It looked welcoming, a large deck wrapped around its simple design. There were a few jeeps already parked there, and a tent erected at the rear.

Alarmed, Paul made sure Mariah was secure in her fanny pack, close to his chest. "Who's here?" He looked at Sigmud accusingly.

"Calm yourself. They are brother and sisters to us. Angelkind." Sigmud smiled, very calm. "You will soon see that many are drawn to us. I have felt them throughout our travels. They know Mariah is here, and want to be near her. Do not be afraid ,Paul. If you were not so tense, you would feel them too, looking for us, hopeful." Even as they parked, another vehicle pulled up.

Michael peered out and saw smoke drifting up from the tent. He could

smell food cooking. "They are gathering," he mumbled, amazed.

Paul felt unsure, and a little overwhelmed. Gathering? "They will lead our enemies right to us."

Chao opened his door to step out. "Let them come. Their chance is over. Mariah no longer has just us, she has an army. No one can touch her or harm her now."

Paul sighed wearily. "Unlike you, I am not so sure of anything. I have seen how something unexpected can happen, despite what we do." He kissed the top of Mariah's head.

Michael nodded. "True Paul, very true. But the reality of all this is, she's in the Creators hands, just as we are. We have no control. All we can do is try our best to earn a good outcome. All we can do, is love this child." As Michael spoke, he realized more deeply just how true his words were.

Chao and Angelo got out, and stretched their legs, breathing in the fresh air. The rushing river lent it's soft music. A raft came into view on the river, and it's occupants tied it to the small dock that led from the deck to the river. Two women got out and walked over to the van. Obviously of native american descent, they smiled shyly. Chao greeted them. "We have come to help," they offered.

Michael's words rested in Paul's mind, and their logic soon rooted itself there. He had to release his fear and distrust, and enjoy this time. It may be the best time of their lives. Forgiveness. He got out of the van and removed Mariah from the fanny pack. He handed her to one of the women. They showered her with brilliant smiles and baby sounds. It was bittersweet to see her in another woman's arms.

Michael got out and accompanied them to the cabin, chatting amiably that it was time to feed the baby. They paid close attention, holding Mariah close.

Paul stared up at the sky, which seemed larger than he'd ever seen it. The sun had set, but the orange hued clouds promised a lovely tomorrow. Angelo stood next to him. "Paul,..how will we know? Can we just assume that little Mariah will be our salvation, and set our souls free? Will we feel different somehow?"

For a few minutes, Paul just looked up at the endless sky. Tempest would have loved this sky,..this place. She couldn't have died for nothing.

Looking at Angelo, he stated,"We just have to trust. That's all."

Chao and Sigmud stood in the open doorway, beckoning to them to come inside. Smiling, Paul nodded toward them. "C'mon. We're needed inside."

They walked together, at ease even as another car pulled up by the deck.

Yes, it promised to be quite a gathering. It was their time. There was the sudden rumble of loud thunder,..or was it the crash of hundreds of Angel wings?

The End

www.ingramcontent.com/pod-product-compliance
Lightning Source LLC
Chambersburg PA
CBHW022005010726

47494CB00003B/902